I0817615

SHOWDOWN AT JULESBURG STATION

Also by Wayne C. Lee and available from Center Point Large Print:

A Stranger in Stirrup
Devil Wire

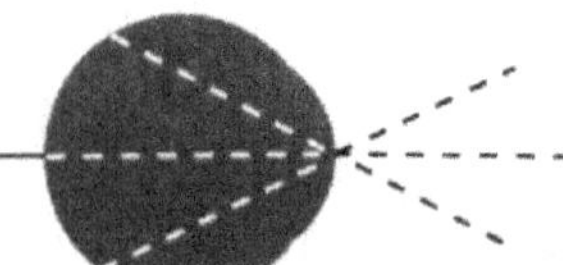

This Large Print Book carries the Seal of Approval of N.A.V.H.

SHOWDOWN AT JULESBURG STATION

Wayne C. Lee

CENTER POINT LARGE PRINT
THORNDIKE, MAINE

This Center Point Large Print edition
is published in the year 2023 by arrangement with
Golden West Inc.

Originally published in the US by Avalon Books.

The text of this Large Print edition is unabridged.
In other aspects, this book may vary
from the original edition.
Printed in the United States of America
on permanent paper sourced using
environmentally responsible foresting methods.
Set in 16-point Times New Roman type.

ISBN 978-1-63808-630-7 (hardcover)
ISBN 978-1-63808-634-5 (paperback)

The Library of Congress has cataloged this record
under Library of Congress Control Number: 2022947599

ONE

Dan Quint shaded his eyes against the April sun and tried to identify the rider charging recklessly toward him. A chill of apprehension trickled over him from the urgency of both horse and rider. Quint's mother came out of the house, wiping her hands on her apron. She held a hand above her eyes as she watched the rider.

"Looks like Judd," she said finally.

Quint nodded, for he had already recognized his stepfather, Judd Hurley. His excitement slowly soured, but his apprehension increased. Judd Hurley always meant trouble for Quint.

Quint had been at his farm in eastern Kansas only a couple of days on this visit. He had seldom returned since the spring of 1854 when his mother had married Judd Hurley. Judd and his son, Blix, two years older than Quint, had moved out to the farm and taken over. Quint, seventeen then, had found himself the target of Judd's meanest moods. Now Quint was twenty-three, and he didn't propose to take any more of Judd's bossing.

"Maybe Blix is in trouble," Quint said almost hopefully.

"Judd wouldn't leave him if he was," Ann said.

Quint knew she was right. Anyway, Judd was

coming from the direction of the pasture, not from town. Blix was probably in town at the saloon where he spent practically all his time, gaining a reputation as a gambler.

Judd's horse was wet with sweat when he brought it to a sliding halt in the yard and threw himself from the saddle. Judd was a big man, standing nearly six feet tall and weighing about two hundred pounds. He lost his hat when he hit the ground, and he stooped to pick it up, jamming it back over iron-gray hair that Quint remembered had been almost jet black when he had first met him.

"What's wrong?" Ann asked as Judd flipped the reins around the short hitchrack in front of the house.

"Jardine!" Judd exploded in his heavy voice. "He's determined to run us off this farm one way or another."

Quint frowned. "What did he do now?"

Sam Jardine's farm was just beyond Hurley's pasture. The two families had been at daggers' points ever since they had settled here.

"The sidewinder caught your horse and cut the tendons on his back legs," Judd said, facing Quint squarely. "I had to kill him."

Quint felt as if a mule had kicked him in the belly. His horse was the one thing he owned that he was really proud of. And it was all he had left after that holdup in the stage station at Prairie

Flats. That horse had cost Quint more than five months' wages. It had both speed and endurance. If it was dead, as Judd was saying, he would find the man responsible and make him wish he had never been born.

"Are you sure it was Jardine?" Quint asked, fighting to control his voice.

Judd nodded. "I don't know of any other man mean enough to do a thing like that. Anyway, your horse is lying right next to the fence between our places."

"You say you had to kill him?"

Again Judd nodded. "With those tendons cut, he would never have been able to walk again. I saved you the misery of shooting him."

"Can I borrow a horse?" Quint asked.

"Sure," Judd said. "I'll saddle one for you."

Quint ran into the house while Judd headed for the corral. He went to his bedroll, which he had tossed in a corner, and took out his gun and belt. He hadn't worn his gun since he had arrived, for he knew his mother didn't like to see him carry it. But he might need it before he got back from this trip.

When he went back outside, Ann Hurley was still in the yard, and Judd was bringing a saddled horse from the barn. Quint would check on his horse; he didn't trust Judd, even in a case like this. If it was the way Judd said it was, then he would hunt down the man who was responsible and make him pay for it. He didn't doubt that the man would be Sam Jardine.

"Why would Jardine cripple my horse?" Quint asked as he took the reins from Judd.

"He's low-down mean, that's why," Judd said. "Maybe he thought he could bluff you and you'd sell out. He knows this farm is in your name, and he aims to get it any way he can. Or maybe he's just striking back at you for that whipping you gave him."

Quint mounted his horse, and his mother reached up to touch his knee. "Don't do anything foolish, Dan. After all, you don't know who did it."

"What kind of talk is that?" Judd demanded angrily. "Nobody but Jardine would do a thing like that. Besides, he's the only one with a reason."

"I'll be careful, Ma," Quint said, nudging the horse into a fast walk.

Once out of the yard, he kicked the horse into a gallop toward the far end of the pasture. If Judd was lying to him, he would go back and thrash him within an inch of his life, something he would relish doing, anyway.

But before he got to the end of the pasture, he saw the horse lying stretched out in the grass. He reined up and dismounted as he saw something in the grass close to the dead horse. He picked up a heavy, bone-handled hunting knife with the initials "S.J." cut in the handle. It wasn't an unusual knife, but it bore Sam Jardine's initials.

Maybe Jardine had been surprised in his dirty work, possibly by Judd, and had dropped the knife in his haste to get away. Or maybe he had left it here deliberately.

A man would have to be vicious, mean to the core, to hurt an animal. Maybe Sam Jardine was. Quint had seen him only a few times in the last six years. The last time had been a couple of days ago when he had ridden in. He had cut across a corner of Jardine's land, and Jardine had taken it as a personal affront. Quint didn't take the kind of abuse that Jardine had heaped on him from any man. He had thoroughly whipped Jardine in the fight that followed.

He had learned later from Judd that the Hurleys and the Jardines had a mutual "no-trespassing" agreement; Jardine had apparently thought Quint was deliberately violating it. Perhaps this horse-crippling was Jardine's way of getting even for the whipping Quint had given him. But if he thought the scales were balanced now, he was going to be surprised.

He wheeled his horse toward the log house of Sam Jardine. He was going to break that no-trespassing agreement again. And that wasn't all he was going to break.

He thundered into Jardine's yard, anger hammering through him. He would make Jardine pay plenty for what he had done. He was sobered a little by the sudden thought that maybe Jardine hadn't done it; maybe the knife had been planted there by someone else. His rage cooled a little. The evidence was convincing, but he would give Jardine a chance to deny it and explain the knife if he could.

A woman came out into the yard when Quint yelled. Quint scowled, "Where's Sam?"

"In town, I think," the woman said. "Is there something I can do for you?"

Quint shook his head and wheeled his horse into the road. The sight of the woman, Sam Jardine's wife, took more of the edge off Quint's rage. He had nothing against Mrs. Jardine. It wasn't her fault that her husband was as poison-mean as a rattler.

It was four miles to town, and as he rode, Quint gradually settled down to straight thinking. He wished he had gone directly to Julesburg after the holdup in the stage station in Prairie Flats. But he had lost his own money in that holdup, and it seemed logical to stop by the farm and get a stake from his stepfather. After all, Judd Hurley was living on Quint's farm. Surely he owed Quint a little for the use of the farm.

Quint had planned to stop only a day to visit his mother and get a stake to go on west to Julesburg. He had been home two days now, and he still didn't have any money. Now he didn't even have a horse to ride.

He couldn't wait much longer. The torn piece of paper in his pocket was like a pointed prod urging him on. He wouldn't rest easy until he had seen the other half of that paper himself.

The death of his horse was a severe setback in his effort to get to Julesburg. But even more, it was like losing a friend. As Quint came in sight of town, his rage began to surge back. He thought of Sam Jardine somewhere in town, probably in a saloon, laughing about the way he had struck at Dan Quint.

Quint rode down the street looking for the horse Jardine had been riding a couple of days before. When he spotted the horse standing in front of a saloon, he reined in beside it and dismounted. Hitching his horse to the rail, he ducked under the bar and went into the saloon, recognizing it as the one in which Blix Hurley spent most of his time gambling.

He stood just inside the door and looked over the half-filled room. He saw Blix sitting at a gambling table with three other men. One, a tall, slim man with blond hair and light gray eyes was looking straight at Quint. Quint returned the stare, feeling a sharp tug of elusive recognition that sent prickly fingers crawling up his spine.

But Quint was looking for Sam Jardine now, and he tore his eyes away from the tall, thin man. Then he saw Jardine sitting at a table close to the door with two others, playing cards. He stepped over to the table and stood glaring down at Jardine.

Jardine looked up from his cards. "Something on your mind, Quint?"

"Plenty," Quint said. "I want pay for my horse."

Jardine frowned. "What horse?"

"The one you butchered with this and left to die," Quint said, and jabbed the knife into the table top, where it stuck, the bone handle quivering.

Jardine slammed his chair backward as he got up. "I didn't butcher your horse!"

"That's your knife, isn't it?" Quint asked, stabbing a finger at the knife still vibrating in the table top.

"Sure it's mine," Jardine said. "But I didn't butcher a horse with it."

"How did it get out there where my horse was cut up?"

"How do I know?" Jardine shouted, his face reddening. He backed off a few steps, glaring at Quint. "No pin-eared saddle bum is going to stand there accusing me of cutting up a horse."

"I am accusing you," Quint said grimly, "unless you can prove you didn't do it."

"I don't have to prove anything to you," Jardine shouted, backing off another step, his right shoulder sagging as his hand inched toward his gun.

"Hold on now!" one of the men at the table

shouted as they both jammed back their chairs and got to their feet.

"Stay out of this, Harve," Jardine said, never taking his eyes off Quint.

Quint hadn't expected this turn of events. At most, he had expected another fist fight with Jardine. But Jardine wasn't thinking in terms of fists now. If it came to guns, Quint decided, there must be only one explanation: Jardine was guilty.

Quint had never drawn a gun on a man before, but if ever there was a man he wanted to kill, it was the man who had cut up his horse.

"I won't be as easy to handle as my horse was," Quint warned.

"I can handle any saddle bum," Jardine snarled.

Then swiftly, as if he couldn't wait another second, Jardine's hand dived for his gun. Quint saw it, and his reaction was almost involuntary.

Quint was fast with a gun, and Jardine wasn't. Quint's gun spoke first. Jardine's gun exploded, the bullet plowing into the floor a yard in front of his feet.

Quint stood as if transfixed as he saw Jardine slump forward and sprawl on the floor. His two companions at the card table rushed forward and knelt beside him. One of them felt for his pulse, then looked up at Quint, shock in his eyes.

"You killed him!" he whispered.

"He drew first," Quint said, glancing around at the others in the saloon. Blix was watching, eager anticipation in his face. His pale-eyed companion seemed more amused than concerned.

"You prodded him into it," the other man beside Jardine said, getting to his feet. "Sam Jardine was not a man to take the kind of accusations you were throwing at him."

"He butchered my horse," Quint said, knowing that this was an argument he could never win. A man was dead, and he had killed him. No reason he could give would sound logical in the face of stark reality.

"He didn't touch your horse," the man said. "He hasn't been out of town since yesterday. He stayed with me last night."

Quint looked sharply at the man, Ben Stollard. Quint knew him well. He was not a man to lie. Quint's horse had been cut up today; Quint had turned him into the pasture himself this morning after feeding him. So, according to Stollard's story, Sam Jardine could not have been guilty of crippling his horse.

"Why didn't he deny it?" Quint demanded, anger and consternation warring within him.

"He did," Stollard said. "At least he denied it as much as Sam Jardine ever denied anything. He wouldn't beg."

"But that knife," Quint said, feeling the rising anger around him, not just in Jardine's two companions but in everyone in the room. "He admitted it was his."

"Sure it was his," Stollard said, stepping around Jardine's body to face Quint. "It was taken from him when he was robbed a week ago. Find the man who had that knife and you'll find the man who took Sam's money. Maybe you're the one."

"He killed Sam; we know that," one man back in the crowd yelled. "I say we ought to string him up right here and now."

The shout that followed warned Quint of the mood pervading the crowd. Sam Jardine had been a popular man; popular enough that the way he had died could drive these men to violent action.

Quint swung his gaze from face to face. He saw the same thing in every one. They would hang him in a minute if someone led the way. And there were two or three men here who were willing to do just that.

Quint had his back to the door, the way he had come in. And he still had his gun in his hand. He realized now that the gun was the only thing that was keeping this crowd from turning into a lynch mob on the spot.

"You're not stringing me up," Quint said, sweeping the crowd with the muzzle of the gun. "I didn't ask for a gunfight. Don't try to follow me or you'll have more than one funeral to handle."

Quint retreated toward the door, fighting to keep from hastily backpedaling. He knew that any show of the fear crawling through him would bring on a mad rush that would overwhelm him.

He kicked open the door and backed through. Once out of sight of the men, he wheeled to his horse standing at the hitchrack and, jerking the reins loose, leaped into the saddle. As men were slamming against the door, he fired a shot into the jamb just above their heads. The faces in the doorway disappeared like magic.

Wheeling his horse, he thundered down the street. He was almost a block from the saloon when the first shot rang out behind him. Bending low over the saddle, he spurred his horse down a side street, putting a building between him and the angry men behind. It would take them a while to get organized to follow him.

Once out of town, Quint reined his horse straight for the farm. He had to get out of eastern Kansas where he hadn't lived for six years. He was only seventeen then. People wouldn't remember him, or if they did, they'd think he had changed. Most of them, when they heard the story the men in the saloon would tell, would quickly tag him as a coldblooded killer. He wouldn't stand a chance in court.

His only chance was to run. He could get lost in that vast expanse that stretched all the way to California. And out there on the South Platte was Julesburg where he had to go, anyway.

Suddenly, it struck him like an iron fist where he had seen that pale-eyed man with Blix; he realized that there was more than just an angry mob back there wanting him dead. Blix's companion was one of the men who had held up the stage office and killed Quint's friend, Joe Linzy. He must know that Linzy had given Quint that torn note. It wasn't by accident that the pale-eyed man was in this country. He would be more determined than anybody in that mob to catch up with Quint.

TWO

Quint saw no sign of pursuit as he pounded cross-country toward the farm. But he didn't fool himself into thinking that they would not follow him. Very likely the law would be with them.

As he rode, he realized what a fool he had been. He had fought Judd's battle for him. It had been Judd and Sam Jardine who had been feuding all these years. Quint's only fight with Jardine had been two days ago on Jardine's land. Still, it had been Quint who had fought Jardine in the showdown battle.

That showdown between Judd Hurley and Sam Jardine had been coming for years. The circumstances that had brought Judd and Jardine together had actually been set in motion on the Oregon Trail back in '52. The accident on Windlass Hill that had taken Herman Quint's life had completely changed every plan that Dan Quint and his mother had made. Quint had often wondered since that day how the nut had happened to come off Herman Quint's wagon wheel just when the wagon was about halfway down Windlass Hill. Since Herman Quint hadn't had such a heavy load, no windlass had been attached to his wagon, and when the wheel came off, there was nothing to prevent the wagon from lurching forward and rolling over. Herman Quint had never had a chance to leap free, and the wagon had rolled over him.

Dan Quint and his widowed mother had gone on to Ft. Laramie with the train, but there they had turned back. Judd Hurley had been wagon boss of the train, but at Ft. Laramie he had found a capable wagon boss and had turned his job over to him. He and his son, Blix, had come back to St. Joseph with Quint and his mother.

Herman Quint, a successful merchant in St. Joseph, had left his wife more money than most widows had. Ann Quint had taken some of that money, bought a farm, and put it in her son's name. The next summer, Judd Hurley had been out at the farm half the time helping young Dan Quint do the work.

Quint had been appreciative of the help until he realized that Judd was only after his mother. Although Dan didn't approve of Judd Hurley's attentions to his mother, he could do nothing to stop them; in the spring of '54, Judd Hurley and Ann Quint were married.

When Hurley moved out to the farm with his son, Quint found himself in a position little better than that of a hired man, even though the farm was in his name. His mother had told him it would be his to do with as he pleased when he was twenty-one. But that had been four years away then. Quint had no intention of staying around and being bossed by Judd Hurley for four long years. So he had packed his few belongings and gone out to make his own way.

He had found work on a ranch and had come back once or twice a year to see his mother. When he turned twenty-one, he considered kicking Judd Hurley and Blix off the farm and working it himself. But his mother, as Judd's wife, would have gone with him. He couldn't kick his own mother out of her home. So he had done nothing, and Judd and Blix remained on the farm while Quint continued to work on ranches wherever he could find a job.

Each time Quint came home, he heard more about the trouble between Judd and Sam Jardine. But it hadn't reached a climax until today. And today, Quint had been in the center of it, not Judd.

Quint realized he had been a fool to come home this time. He should have known that Judd would not stake him to the trip to Julesburg. He would have been better off heading west, living off the land as he went.

But what was done was done. He had stopped; he had killed Sam Jardine; and now he had to run. If he had headed straight for Julesburg, he could have been many miles out on the prairie now. He would have been much closer to finding out what his friend, Joe Linzy, had meant for him to know when he gave him that torn piece of paper with just half a set of instructions. Quint's half would make no sense to him until he found the other half. And that half, according to Joe Linzy's dying words, was in Gilda Ryan's hands in Julesburg.

Behind him now, Quint saw a cloud of dust rising. The men of town were getting organized and were on his trail. He lifted the reins and urged his weary horse to a faster clip. He had a good lead that kept him out of sight of his pursuers; he had to keep it.

He considered wheeling away from his course and bypassing the farm while he could still do it without his pursuers knowing. But he needed a fresh horse. And he had to tell his mother what had happened and why he was riding on. He didn't care about Judd Hurley.

So Quint urged his horse straight ahead. When Quint got to the farm, his horse was lathered, its sides heaving. He swung down and ran into the house, where he found his mother and Judd, almost as if they had been waiting for him.

"What happened?" Ann Hurley demanded.

"I found Sam Jardine's knife close to my horse," Quint explained. "I went after Jardine and found him in town. He wouldn't talk reason, just drew on me. I killed him. Now the whole town is after me."

Judd Hurley shook his head sadly. "That's bad," he said. "Even though Jardine was a skunk, he had a lot of friends. You'll have to clear out fast."

"That's what I intend to do," Quint said.

He ran into the room where he had been sleeping. Most of his things were already in his bedroll. It took only a minute to cram the rest into it. He carried the roll out to the living room.

"I'll have to have a horse," he said.

Judd scratched his chin. "I'm mighty short on horses. Things haven't been going well here on the farm."

"I can't get away on foot," Quint said, irritated.

He had done Judd a favor by eliminating Jardine. Judd's way of showing his appreciation was to refuse him a horse. He knew that Quint would have little chance of escaping without one.

"Was it a fair fight?" Ann Hurley asked.

"Of course it was, Ma," Quint said. "I didn't want a gunfight. But Jardine seemed to think that was the only way to settle it after I'd accused him of butchering my horse. He drew first."

"Then you don't have to run," Ann said. "Stay here and prove it was a fair fight."

"How could he do that?" Judd asked. "If he had to run to get out of town, you can bet those who saw the fight will testify against him. I'll let you have a horse, Dan. Take the one you rode out. It's already saddled."

"Take some bread and meat with you," Ann said, quickly gathering up some food and putting it in a sack. "And here's a letter that came for you." She held it out to him. "Bill Jones, our neighbor to the north, brought out the mail while you were gone. This was in it."

Quint took the sack, then stuffed the letter in his pocket. "Thanks, Ma. I'll read it later."

He turned and ran toward the horse in the yard. The horse was already winded, but if he used him carefully, he might make better time than by stopping to catch and saddle another. He had to get away before the posse got close enough to see in which direction he rode.

"Where are you going, Dan?" Ann called after him.

"West," Quint said. "Maybe to the gold fields in Colorado." He didn't want to tell anybody, not even his own mother, about his mission to Julesburg.

In the saddle now, he reined out of the yard, lifting a hand in farewell to his mother. He shot a look toward town. There was nothing on the road as far as he could see. But hills cut off his vision a short distance away.

He reined toward the creek where trees would screen his movements. Once in the trees, he turned west, following the creek upstream. After he got well away from the farm, he would angle northwest to the road leading from St. Joseph toward the great wide country that stretched out for hundreds of unmarked miles.

Out there somewhere beyond the forks of the Platte was Julesburg. And somewhere in

Julesburg, according to Joe Linzy's story, was a girl named Gilda Ryan. She had the other half of the note Linzy had given Quint. When these two halves were put together, Quint and Gilda Ryan would know where a fortune was hidden, Linzy had said.

Quint hadn't really known Joe Linzy well. He had met him only a month ago on the ranch where he had worked close to Prairie Flats. Linzy was a loner, but somehow he had warmed up to Quint; they had been buddies for the month they worked together.

Then Linzy had quit his job and told Quint he was going back to Julesburg to marry his girl, Gilda Ryan. Quint had gone with him to the stage station, figuring on riding on to another job after he had seen Linzy off. He had the promise from a friend of a job close to Topeka.

But at the stage station, while they were waiting for the stage, two masked bandits had suddenly appeared. Quint had thought it was a simple holdup. But Linzy had seemed to know better from the moment the bandits appeared.

The two outlaws had immediately concentrated on Linzy. But when they got close, Linzy had lunged forward ripping the mask from the tall man's face. Quint had gotten only a glimpse of his face before a gun barrel had cracked down against his own head.

When he came to, only the stationmaster was in

the station with Quint. The stage had not arrived yet. But both the bandits and Joe Linzy had disappeared. The stationmaster had been knocked out, but he had already recovered. He couldn't tell Quint anything about his partner, however. They had all disappeared before he regained consciousness.

Quint had stumbled outside and found Linzy not far from the station. He had been beaten and was obviously dying. He wanted to tell Quint something, and Quint listened.

Linzy had been beaten around the face and mouth so badly that the words he spoke were barely understandable. But Quint made out most of what he said. Mumbling, he instructed Quint to take one of his boots. Underneath the insole of the boot, Quint found a piece of paper.

The paper was half of a note, indicating, Linzy said, where a cache of money was hidden. Gilda Ryan in Julesburg had the other half. Linzy made Quint promise to deliver the piece of paper to Gilda. They could share the money they found.

Quint had a dozen questions to ask Linzy: about the money, Gilda, why he had given her only half, instead of all, the note. But before he could ask any of those questions, Joe Linzy had died.

Quint had tried to make sense of the note. But the paper had been torn from top to bottom so that Quint's half contained only partial sentences that made little sense. He thought of throwing it away. After all, he had known Joe Linzy only a month. When Quint tried to remember something definite about him, he realized that Linzy had said practically nothing about his past.

But a promise to a dying man was something almost sacred. Quint knew he would deliver that note to Gilda Ryan in Julesburg if he could find her. His job close to Topeka would bring him no more than the job he had been working at. But then he discovered that he didn't even have his wages from his previous job. The bandits had robbed him as well as the stage station.

Quint's next thought was to stop by his home and get a stake from Judd Hurley. Then he would go on to Julesburg. From there, he wasn't sure what he would do. It would depend on what the note led him to. If he got nothing for his trouble, he might come back to his job in Kansas or go on to the gold fields in Colorado. The stories he had been hearing about them drew him like a magnet.

But first he would find Gilda Ryan and determine what the note said. Why hadn't Joe Linzy given Gilda all the note if he wanted her to have the money, as he obviously had?

He thought of the slim man with Blix back in the saloon in town. His was the face behind the mask that Linzy had jerked off back in the stage station in Prairie Flats. That was the man that Quint had sworn he would kill if he ever got the chance. Joe Linzy had not been a close friend of Quint's, but he had been his partner at the time he was killed. Quint felt driven to avenge his death if possible. If the man had shot Linzy in a fair fight, Quint would have been content to let it go. But he had beaten Linzy to death as he would a snake. Quint could never let that go unavenged.

Suddenly a rider appeared among the trees ahead. Quint reined up, his hand streaking to his gun. But the other man already had a gun in his hand. Quint's hand came back to the horn of his saddle, but his anger soared as he recognized Blix Hurley.

"What's the idea of coming at me with a gun in your hand?" he demanded.

"I was afraid you might be jumpy enough to have an itchy trigger finger," Blix said.

"I might be, at that," Quint said. "What's on your mind?"

"That horse," Blix said. "I just came past the house. Pa says he needs it."

"He said I could have it," Quint shot back. "He's been living on my land free for six years. The least he can do is give me a horse."

Blix shook his head. "He can do less. He wants that horse back."

"He's not going to get him," Quint said.

Blix waved the gun easily. "I think he will. If I have to wing you, I'll do it, then turn you over to that mob in town. They'll swing you higher than a kite."

"You're a double-dealing skunk, Blix," Quint said, fighting his rage. "How do you expect me to get away from that mob if I'm afoot?"

Blix shrugged. "That's your worry, not mine. My worry is getting that horse back to Pa. Reckon I ought to take you back to town and turn you in for murdering Sam Jardine. But I'll let somebody else have that honor. They'll have no trouble finding you. Now get out of that saddle."

Quint considered trying for his gun. He would feel no reluctance at shooting Blix Hurley. He had hated Blix, he thought, ever since he had first fought with him on the trail eight years ago. But he knew he would never reach his gun. Blix was anticipating just such a move. He had to do what Blix said and wait for a chance to even the score. Slowly he swung off his horse.

"Someday, Blix, we'll meet when you won't hold all the cards."

Blix laughed softly. "I doubt it. There are a lot of men out looking for you right now. After they find you, I'm afraid I won't have the pleasure of seeing you alive again."

"Do I get my bedroll?"

"Sure," Blix said. "I've got a good bed at home with a roof over my head." He laughed again. "It may be in your name now, but the only land a dead man can claim is a plot six by three."

Quint took the bedroll off the back of the saddle, trying desperately to find some way to turn the tables. But Blix was making sure that he got no chance.

"Now step back," Blix ordered when Quint had his bedroll. "Take your gun out of the holster real easy and toss it over against that tree."

Quint obeyed, realizing that Blix apparently was going to leave him his gun. He hadn't expected even that much. Blix probably thought that Quint's fighting the posse would hasten his hanging once they captured him.

Quint stood by helplessly as Blix picked up the reins of the horse and led him away.

THREE

When Blix had disappeared into the trees, Quint ran for his gun. But there was nothing to shoot at now. He started to run after Blix, but an echoing laugh from far ahead stopped him. Blix was already out of range of Quint's six-gun. Quint caught a glimpse of him through the trees now and then. He would speed up even more once he reached the open prairie.

Choking back his rage, Quint turned into the trees again, walking ahead on the course he had planned to take with his horse. He wondered how far he would get before the posse overtook him. If Blix didn't tell any of the men from town where he had left him, they might not find him for a while. They wouldn't expect him to be on foot.

Quint guessed he was nearly ten miles from the farm when darkness began to creep in among the trees along the creek. He was thinking about finding a place to spend the night when he caught his heel on a tree root and fell headlong.

Jarred by the fall, he got to his feet slowly, only to discover that he had torn the heel off his boot. He scowled. It was going to be a job getting that boot heel nailed back on. It was a cinch he could not walk in a boot with no heel.

He found a place to spend the night, but he didn't start a fire. That might be just what his pursuers would be looking for. He ate a cold supper of the bread and boiled ham his mother had given him.

Suddenly he remembered the letter she had handed him as he was leaving the farm. He pulled it out of his pocket and opened it. By the fading light, he made out the scrawled words on the page:

> If you hand over the note Linzy said you had, you'll live a while. The sheriff didn't give us time to get it at the stage station. If you don't turn it over to us, you'll get what Linzy got.

The letter bore no signature, but in Quint's mind it was signed. It had to have come from the slim young man with the pale eyes who had been playing cards with Blix Hurley in the saloon. The sheriff must have run him off at the stage station in Prairie Flats, but somehow he had traced Quint to his farm. And he was going to get that half note some way. Quint wondered if he knew it was just half a note. Probably he thought Quint had the entire thing. Linzy must have told the two killers that Quint had it in the hope that they would let him live. But it had been a vain hope.

In the fading light, Quint fished out the

crumpled paper that he had dug out of Linzy's boot. The light was so faint now that Quint could barely read the writing. But he had studied that note so long that he knew it by heart.

> The money
> floor in t
> corner of
> cabin nex
> station. D
> see you g

Quint studied the note for a long while, trying to fill in the other part of it. He had no idea whether it had been a wide paper or a narrow one. It would make a lot of difference just how many words were on the other half. He guessed there was some money hidden under a floor of a cabin somewhere. But where the cabin was would be a mystery to Quint until he saw the other half of the note which Gilda Ryan was supposed to have.

He had no idea how much money was involved but he had to assume it was plenty or the pale-eyed man would not be going to such extremes to get his hands on it. The man thought he had this note, so Quint's life wasn't worth a plugged nickel if he got careless. The man had killed once to get it; he would kill again if necessary.

He knew he would never give him this half note. He wanted to kill that man for the way he had murdered Joe Linzy, not give him the key to a fortune. Even if he did give him this half note, the chances were that the man would think Quint was still keeping the other half; and he would then be more determined than ever to kill him to get it.

No, he would keep the note and give it to Gilda Ryan as he had promised Linzy. No matter what happened, he wouldn't let the pale-eyed gunman get it.

He looked at the small piece of paper, trying to think where he could hide it so that nobody would find it. If the sheriff hadn't interrupted the men back at Prairie Flats, they would probably have found it eventually in Linzy's boot.

As darkness settled down, Quint turned his attention to the boot heel that he would have to nail back on. Suddenly an idea struck him. If he could hollow out a spot in that heel and put the note in there, then nail the heel back on his boot, no one would be likely to find it.

Digging his knife out of his pocket, he began working on the heel. It was slow work, for the heel was made of hard wood. But in time he had a small hollow in the center of the heel. He folded the note into a small pad and pressed it into the hollow place. Then he fitted the heel back on the boot.

Although it was almost totally dark now, he found a rock he could use as a boot last and another he could use as a hammer and tapped the heel back on the boot. At the first opportunity, he would have to secure the heel better. But it was the best he could do now.

He rolled up in his blankets and tried to sleep. But his mind was seething. He had to find a way to get to Julesburg with that half note. That letter he had received had crystallized his determination.

He recalled that the road west from St. Joseph crossed this stream a few miles ahead. He would go to that crossing, he decided, and either hook on with a train going west or steal a horse from some outfit and ride west alone.

With that decision made, his thoughts returned to the day just past. If Jardine had not been out of town since the day before, how had his knife gotten out there by Quint's horse?

Suddenly, now that he had time to really think about it, the answer struck Quint. The men had said that Jardine had been robbed the week before. Quint had heard that himself from Judd Hurley, who had said that Jardine had sold some cattle in St. Joseph and had been held up on the way home.

Now it all began to fit together. Who would profit most by robbing Jardine or by seeing him killed now? Judd Hurley. Judd had known that nothing could stir up Quint like cutting up his horse. He must have felt sure that Quint would go after Jardine without asking too many questions, especially if he found Jardine's knife at the scene. That knife beside the dead horse had been the lighted fuse designed to explode in a fight between Quint and Jardine. It mattered little to Judd Hurley which man won.

If Quint won, it would mean that Jardine would be out of Judd's way, and it was likely that Judd could eventually acquire Jardine's farm. Not only that, but Quint was almost certain to get into serious trouble with the law.

That would play right into Judd's hands. The farm where he lived was in Quint's name and until Quint was eliminated, Judd couldn't get title to the farm. Besides that, Judd hated Quint, had hated him from the time they had met. And Quint returned the feeling in full measure.

Judd must feel sure now that the law would catch up with Quint, especially since he was afoot. When the law was finished with Quint, Judd would have little trouble getting title to the farm.

On the other hand, if Sam Jardine had killed Quint, it would have been Jardine in trouble with the law. Jardine wouldn't have run like Quint was doing. He had a farm and a wife here. So Judd would have just sat back and waited for the law to do its work. Either way, Judd must have felt sure that he had a good chance of getting both Quint's and Jardine's farms in due time.

Quint was awake before sunup and out of his blankets. He ate a cold breakfast again, for he couldn't risk a fire. If Blix had found the posse, the law would know now that he was afoot. It would be only a matter of time until the hunters found him.

Staying in the trees, he moved on upstream, watching the hills on either side. Once he saw three riders off to his right, and he guessed that they were looking for him.

He fought down an impulse to go back, settle his score once and for all with Judd Hurley, take one of his horses, and then head for Julesburg. But he knew that would be the most foolish move he could make. There were men back there just waiting for him to make one mistake. And the pale-eyed man was back there somewhere, too. If Quint wanted to stay alive and out of jail, his only chance was to go ahead, steal a horse or hook on with a train going to Julesburg. He had the feeling he could hurt the pale-eyed man most by getting this half note to Gilda Ryan at Julesburg.

It was after noon when he reached the ford where the trail out of St. Joseph crossed the little stream. From there, the trail angled off toward a junction with the road coming up from Independence and Leavenworth on its way to Nebraska Territory. He had to have a horse. And the only place where he would have much chance of getting one was from a train passing by. He knew that some trains camped by the stream their first night out of St. Joseph.

Quint found a spot where anyone riding past was unlikely to see him and curled up for a nap. It could be several days before a train came by. Not as many people started west from St. Joseph as from Independence or Leavenworth. If a train didn't come soon, he would have to change his plans. He didn't have enough food to last him more than another day. He had to get a horse, even if he had to risk going back to some farm to steal one.

He roused with the sun well down in the sky. For a moment, he could not think what had wakened him. Then he heard the creak of wagons, the jangle of chains, and the weary shouts of drivers. Luck was with him. A train was coming.

Quint crawled to a place where he could see the activity without being seen. From this spot he watched more than twenty wagons roll down the gentle slope to the creek and splash across it. There the leader, riding a big black horse, waved the wagons into camp.

Quint kept his position as teams were unhitched and supper fires started. It was almost dark before he stirred. That big black horse that the leader had been riding had attracted his eye. It looked like it had speed and endurance.

But as Quint started to move out of the trees, a

man suddenly appeared in the dusk immediately ahead of him. He was holding a chunk of tree limb above his head.

"Just hold it right there, fellow," the man said, waving the limb threateningly. "Where are you headed?"

Quint stopped. The man obviously had no gun. Quint didn't want to hurt anyone. And if he pulled a gun, he would have to hurt this man or at least let the whole train know he was here, a fugitive and ready to fight.

"I'm heading west; maybe Colorado, maybe California," Quint said.

The man stared at him for a moment. "I thought at first you was an Injun. What happened to you? Miss out on hooking up with a train?"

Quint nodded, thinking quickly. "I heard about this outfit, but I was just too late to latch onto it. Thought I might catch up with it out here."

The man stared through the deepening darkness at Quint. "Walk all the way from St. Joe?"

"Most of the way," Quint said. "Feet's plenty sore, too."

"Reckon they would be. Come on. I'll take you to Tom Letcher. He's our wagon boss. Reckon you know that, though, or you wouldn't have been trying to catch up with us."

Quint nodded, wondering if he would be able to get away with this pretense. He had never heard of Tom Letcher, but maybe he could convince the people of this train that he had planned to go west with Letcher's outfit.

Tom Letcher was a big man, over six feet tall and weighing at least two hundred pounds. He had sandy hair and a gray-sprinkled beard that bristled under his penetrating gaze.

"Where's your horse?" he demanded when Quint had told him his story.

"Got held up back a piece. Lost my horse and everything I had except my bedroll and gun."

"Took your money, too?"

"I'm flat broke," Quint said with a shrug.

"How do you figure to go with us with no money to pay your way?" Letcher asked.

"I was hoping I could work enough to pay for my keep."

Letcher scratched his chin. "I could use an errand boy. I know that's a kid's job, but if you want to go along bad enough, I reckon you'll do it."

Quint nodded. "You've got yourself a flunkey."

Quint put his bedroll in the wagon Letcher pointed out and came back to get orders. He didn't particularly like the idea of being camp flunkey. But maybe that would be a good thing. A flunkey running errands around camp would hardly be suspected of killing a man. Some of these people had probably heard about the killing there while they were outfitting.

As Quint worked around camp, he listened to

the talk among the men. But all he heard was the usual excited talk about the fortunes they were going to make once they got to the promised land.

Quint found a last and fastened his boot heel on solidly before he rolled up in his blankets for the night. If the men from St. Joseph who were searching for him knew that he had been set afoot by the Hurleys, they might suspect that he would try to hook on with a train going west. Quint would have to keep on the alert; they might search this train.

But morning came and the people broke camp and got on the road without any visitors. Day after day, the wagon train moved on, passing into Nebraska Territory without a single challenge. They reached the Platte and camped outside Ft. Kearny.

Now the talk of the men turned to the danger of Indians. There was trouble on the plains, and from this point on they could expect to run into it at any time. Men came out from Ft. Kearny and talked to Tom Letcher. Quint stayed out of sight while the visitors were present. It was unlikely that they would be looking for him or even recognize him if they were, but Quint was taking no chances. He couldn't quell the feeling that if the law abandoned the search, Judd Hurley would take it up in order to drag him back to St. Joseph to stand trial. Hurley wanted to see him hang. And there was the pale-eyed gunman. Quint knew he would never abandon the search.

It was a long, lonely stretch from Ft. Kearny west up the Platte to the next sign of civilization, Julesburg. Some of the people wanted to take the Lower Crossing and go up the North Platte by way of Ash Hollow. But others complained they were low on supplies, and they had heard that Jules Beni's trading post at the budding town of Julesburg sold them.

Tom Letcher listened to the arguments and decided in favor of the Upper Crossing, a mile beyond the Julesburg station.

"We won't lose much time," he said, "because we'll avoid having to go down Windlass Hill into Ash Hollow. They say the Upper Crossing is no worse than this one. Probably most of you will find something you need at Julesburg, anyway."

That suited Quint. He could stay with the train until it got to Julesburg. Maybe, if he found nothing holding him in Julesburg after he delivered that half note to Gilda Ryan, he would go on with the train. The more distance he put between himself and the law back in eastern Kansas, the better he would like it.

So the wagons went past the Lower Crossing and moved up the river a few miles to camp. The next night they camped close to the town of Julesburg, about a mile below the spot where the wagons would cross the South Platte the next day.

They were nearly a half mile from the few buildings that made up the new town. Quint looked around for Tom Letcher. He would have to borrow a horse to ride into town.

He spotted the wagon boss just building a fire to start his supper. Quint was almost to him when he saw two riders coming from town toward the train.

It was almost dark, and Quint couldn't see them well, but the caution that had become so much a part of him drove him back into the shadows behind the wagon where Tom Letcher was working. Letcher continued with his supper, getting his stew in the kettle and the fire burning brightly before the two riders reached him.

"They tell me you're the wagon boss," one man said.

Quint was startled at the familiarity of that voice. He eased around to the rear of the wagon where he could see the men without being seen. He sucked in his breath sharply and his hand dropped automatically to his gun.

One man was rather short and heavy, sitting in the saddle like a loose sack of grain. But the other was tall and slim. The light from the fire touched the blond hair that stuck out from under his hat. Quint could imagine how those faded eyes were studying Tom Letcher. The pale-eyed gunman had caught up with Quint again.

FOUR

Quint eased his gun into his hand as he watched the two riders with Tom Letcher. The pale-eyed man would be inquiring about Quint. Since Quint had not even changed his name when he joined the train, Letcher would have no trouble identifying him. Quint debated his next move if Letcher admitted that he was in the train.

He could leap out into the open and he would have the drop on the pale-eyed killer. He had been looking for an opportunity like this. But Quint was sure from what he already knew of the gunman's determination that he wouldn't throw up his hands and beg for mercy. There would be gunplay, and that could be disastrous in this closely packed camp.

On the other hand, he could sneak away into the shadows and hide where the killer couldn't find him. He might even go into Julesburg. But sneaking away from a fight went against his grain. So he stood in the shadows and waited, his gun held in readiness.

Tom Letcher looked up from the stew he was stirring. "I'm ramrodding this outfit," he said. "Something I can do for you?"

"I reckon there is," the pale-eyed man said. "I'm Cole Fray and this is my sidekick, Russ

Spark. We're looking for a man. Been looking for him for quite a while. He's about 23, weighs around 175. Gray eyes and brown hair, and he carries a gun."

Letcher rubbed his chin. "That description could fit a lot of men," he said. "Is there some special reason why you want to find this one?"

"There sure is. He killed a man back in eastern Kansas."

"That's a long ways off," Letcher said. "What makes you think he might be here?"

"His stepfather told us he thought he might head for the gold fields at Denver. We figured he'd come this way. Too much Indian trouble on the Smoky Hill trail. So we came here to Julesburg quick as we could and have been checking every train that passes. He was afoot unless he stole a horse somewhere. But we figure he probably hooked up with a train going west."

"Like looking for a grain of wheat in a desert, I reckon," Letcher said. "A man like that could be in a thousand different places."

"You're not telling us anything we don't know," Fray said wearily. "But there's a good reward. Have you seen anything of him?"

Quint waited breathlessly for Letcher to answer, his fingers tightening on his gun. Surely Letcher had no doubt that the man they were seeking was his camp flunkey. Letcher had questioned Quint once about his habit of wearing a gun all his waking hours, but he didn't press the subject. Every man in the train kept a gun within reach most of the time while traveling through this desolate country.

"Maybe you ought to tell me a little more about this man," Letcher said slowly. "What's his name, and just what kind of a brutal murder did he commit that would make the law come this far after him?"

"His name is Dan Quint," Fray said. "But it ain't likely that he'd use that name even if you ran into him. Quint stirred up a fight with Sam Jardine by accusing him of crippling his horse when he hadn't done it at all. When Jardine reached for his gun, Quint shot him."

"If this other man reached for his gun, it sounds like a fair fight," Letcher said slowly. "You sure the law wants him?"

"The law wants him, all right," Fray said. "But it's not the law that's offering the reward for him. It's his stepfather, Judd Hurley. Hurley swears that Quint made off with a lot of his money and he wants it back."

Quint wondered just how much of what Fray was saying was the truth. He didn't doubt that Hurley had offered a reward for him. But if he had, it would be secretly and just to individuals like Cole Fray. He would never make public his desire to get rid of Quint. The reward would be payable only on proof of Quint's death; Quint would wager odds on that. Of course that would fit neatly into Fray's plans. Quint marveled at how easily Fray had kept from revealing his own personal interests. So far as he had made known, he was merely on a mission for Judd Hurley.

Quint was positive that Fray and Spark had not chosen Julesburg by chance as a base for checking out passing wagon trains. Fray seemed to know a lot about Joe Linzy, including his having given the note to Quint. He surely must know about Gilda Ryan in Julesburg. He probably guessed that Quint would seek out Gilda, but Quint doubted if he knew that she had half of Linzy's note of instructions.

"Looks to me," Letcher said finally, "like you're a couple of bounty hunters who ain't real sure the man you're after is guilty of a crime."

"Oh he killed that man, all right," Fray said. "And Hurley swears he stole his money. You haven't told us yet whether you've seen him."

Letcher shook his head. "Don't reckon I've seen any man I'd want to turn over to you two."

Fray sighed, but his eyes continued to dart over the surrounding wagons. "Didn't figure we'd find him. Looks like we missed him somewhere. Reckon we might as well quit looking. Thanks, anyway."

The two men reined their horses out of the circle of wagons and headed for the few buildings of town. Quint watched them go, then went around to the fire where Tom Letcher was starting to ladle up some stew.

"Thanks, Tom," he said.

"Why didn't you tell me what you'd done?" Letcher asked without looking up.

"Didn't figure that would help me get a ride west," Quint said.

"You're right about that. I wouldn't take in a killer, even if he didn't mean to be one. I covered up for you tonight because I felt there was something fishy about those two. Did you steal your stepfather's money?"

"No," Quint said. "I told you I was broke, and I was. In fact, it was Judd Hurley who sent my stepbrother out to take my horse away from me. That's why I was afoot when I hooked on with you."

"Why does he want you back so bad?"

"I don't figure he does want me back," Quint said. "But he'd like to have me dead. He set up that fight between me and Jardine because he was afraid to face Jardine himself. We were both framed."

Letcher nodded. "That sounds more like the truth than what those fellows were saying. Anyway, it looks like you're free of him now. So this will be a good place for you to drop off."

"You don't want me along now?" Quint asked.

"You're bound to make me say it right out, ain't you? I don't want a killer along with me, no matter whether he's a killer by choice or by accident. There's a town here. Maybe you can get a job. It's also a junction of trails. You can hook on with another outfit going to California or to Denver."

Quint nodded. "I was thinking some of going to the Cherry Creek diggings, anyway." He held out his hand. "Thanks, Tom, for bringing me this far and for covering for me tonight."

Letcher shook his hand, then motioned to a pan. "Grab a plate and eat."

When supper was over, Quint rolled into his blankets in his usual spot under the wagon. But he couldn't sleep. He had intended to go into Julesburg, but he had toyed with the idea of going on to California with Letcher's train. Now that idea was out.

He thought about Cole Fray. There had been some vital connection between Fray and Joe Linzy that Quint had known nothing about until that day at the Prairie Flats stage station. Linzy had been engaged to marry Gilda Ryan. Surely Fray knew about Gilda, too.

Would Fray stay in Julesburg, or would he give up his search and go back east as he had hinted? If he went back, Quint's task in Julesburg would be greatly simplified. If he didn't, Quint would have Cole Fray to deal with, probably before he could get to Gilda Ryan.

Then there was the problem of eating. Quint

would have to get work or find Gilda quickly and share the fortune their completed note was supposed to reveal.

He was out of his blankets before daylight, rolled his belongings into his bedroll, then slipped out of camp.

He stopped a short distance from camp where he could watch the town when daylight came. Cole Fray and Russ Spark had ridden toward Julesburg last night. Very likely they were staying some place in town. If they were going to ride on today, Quint wanted to give them a chance to go before he showed up.

Dawn came. Behind him the camp came alive as preparations were made to cross the river. Quint stayed out of sight of the camp. If he were seen, questions would be asked. The fewer questions asked, the better off he would be. Let Tom Letcher explain his disappearance any way he chose. Likely he would tell everybody that Quint had left the train to go to Denver.

The sun rose and the wagons moved out to the bank of the crossing. In town, there was some stirring as men shuffled around in the streets. Quint saw two men come out of a huge building that he guessed to be a hotel or boarding house. They went to a barn and got horses, then rode out, heading east down the river. That would be Fray and Spark.

When they were out of sight, Quint rose and

walked into town. Julesburg was neither a big town nor would its reputation make a preacher smile. He stood at the end of the new street and surveyed the few buildings. Close to the wagon road was Jules Beni's trading post. It was also, according to the sign tacked over the door, the "Leavenworth & Pike's Peak Express" station and the pony express station.

Behind the station was a big barn and corrals, and across from it was a warehouse. Farther down toward the river was the biggest building in town with a boarding-house sign on its front. Across from it was a blacksmith shop. Quint imagined that it got plenty of business since it was the first one he had seen since leaving Ft. Kearny.

Beyond the blacksmith shop was a smaller building that looked like a general store, and beyond it was a pool hall. Across from the pool hall was a long building that bore the words "Saloon—Dance Hall" on its front. There were a few other buildings beyond these, but Quint couldn't see what they were.

Quint wondered where he would find Gilda Ryan. And where, in a town like this, could he find work? He decided it might be a smart move to look for work first and do some cautious inquiring about Gilda. A blunder now might prove costly.

He headed toward the trading post. There were two freighters inside when Quint entered. Quint guessed they were buying supplies, and grain for their mules which were standing outside, hitched to big wagons.

Behind the counter was a dark-skinned man who looked shorter than he really was because of his massive build. His bright eyes sparkled like those of a weasel as he flipped a glance at Quint coming through the door, then turned back to his customers.

Quint waited until the two freighters were gone; then he moved up to the counter.

"What are you looking for?" the big man asked, sizing up Quint with those bright eyes.

"Work," Quint said.

The big man frowned. "People come here to buy stuff." His scowl darkened. "Get kicked off a train or something?"

"I hitched a ride this far," Quint said, avoiding the question. "Now I need work to earn some money."

"I ain't hiring anybody unless he agrees to stay a while. I hire somebody and train him, then he heads for the gold fields on Cherry Creek."

"I figure on staying a while if I get a good job," Quint said. There was a job available here. He had to get it. It might be the only one in town.

"Particular about the kind of work you do?" the big man asked skeptically.

"I'm not afraid of work," Quint said. "Try me and see."

The big man rubbed a stubbly chin. "Maybe I will. I had a kid here who was working pretty good until he took a wild notion yesterday to head for the gold fields. What's your name?"

"Dan Quint."

"I'm Jules Beni," the big man said. "I own this trading post. I'm stationmaster and agent for the overland stage and pony-express stations. There's plenty of work to do when a stage comes in. Teams to change, customers to wait on. And everybody is in a hurry. You'll get your tail worked off then. And you'd better have the fresh horse saddled and ready when the express rider comes through. You'll clerk in the store when you're not working with the horses. Is that clear?"

Quint nodded. It was clear he would have plenty of work to do. A man like Jules Beni would not hire someone, then let him stand around doing nothing, even if there was nothing to do.

"Anybody else work here?" he asked.

"Mike tends to the horses," Jules said. "But he'll need help when the stage comes in, and he may need help for the express rider. He's slower than a turtle in winter. Look around the store. Some prices are marked. If they're not marked, ask me. And remember what I tell you."

Quint knew that he was in for a rough time working for Jules, but he suspected that it would be an exciting job. Any news from the east or west would come into this station first.

"Where you going to live?" Jules asked.

"Hadn't considered," Quint said. "I see there's a boarding house in town."

Jules nodded. "About the only place to stay. You get a room there and whatever Mrs. Ketrick charges you, I'll give you that much and fifty cents a day more."

Jules started arranging things on a shelf, leaving Quint to start work. His first job, he knew, was to learn the prices charged by Jules for everything in the trading post. And Jules had a big inventory. Quint was surprised that a man could offer such a variety of things this far from a source of supply.

At noon, Jules gave Quint half an hour to get his dinner and get back to work. Quint hurried over to the boarding house and rented a room by the week, although he wasn't sure he would stay that long. Mrs. Ketrick, the thin, wiry woman who ran the place, complained that the food she had cooked was for the people on the stage due in less than an hour, but she took out enough to feed Quint. He wanted to ask about Gilda Ryan but got no chance.

Quint found the excitement he expected when the stage came in. Before the stage was due to arrive he had helped Mike Shield, the old man who tended to the horses, get the four fresh horses ready to put on the stage. There was no great hurry, Mike said, because the stage stopped here to let the passengers eat their dinner at the boarding house.

Quint said little while the stage was at the station, but he listened for any news from the east. There was talk of Indian scares along the line and of the political unrest in the east. One man declared there would be war before spring if people elected the radical, Abraham Lincoln.

Two express riders came by during the day, one going each way. Quint got a better chance to find out things from them because this was a home station where riders as well as horses were changed. The only things that had to be transferred in a hurry were the mail pouches.

But he heard nothing about Sam Jardine's death. A thing like that, he decided, was buried in more important things this far out on the frontier. Nor was there any mention of Fray and Spark who had been staying in town. Apparently, no one had bothered to inquire about their business or if they had, their answer had seemed too insignificant to remember.

When Quint was dismissed for the day, he turned up the street of the town. Mrs. Ketrick had said that supper would be at eight. He had half an hour before that—time enough, perhaps, to locate Gilda Ryan.

Grass was still struggling to grow in many places in the street. Only a year or two ago, this had been nothing but prairie, Quint thought. Jules' trading post had been the only establishment along this river for miles in either direction.

Even though the sun was down, the general store appeared to be open. The blacksmith shop was just closing its big front door. The pool hall and saloon farther down the street were both open and showed no sign of closing. A wagon train was camped out south of town, and likely these two establishments hoped to get some business from the train before the evening was gone.

Quint ignored the pool hall and the saloon and turned toward the store. He wondered how Jules liked having competition here in his own town. Jules had impressed Quint as being a jealous, wild-tempered man. In memorizing the prices, Quint had concluded that Jules was charging the highest price that customers would pay for every item in his trading post.

When Quint stepped inside the store, a man and a girl who were behind the counter watched him closely.

"Something we can do for you?" the girl asked.

"Just looking over the town," Quint said.

"You from the wagon train south of town?" the man asked.

Quint shook his head. "I'm working for Jules at the trading post."

"Oh," the girl said, and Quint could feel the coolness that fringed the word.

"I take it you don't approve of Jules," Quint said, moving closer where he could see the girl better in the dim light.

She was about nineteen or twenty, Quint guessed. She was nearly a foot shorter than Quint and weighed no more than a hundred pounds. But her brown eyes held a spark suggesting an inner fire that would make up for her lack of size.

"Jules charges outlandish prices," the girl said.

Quint nodded. "I noticed that today. Are yours any better?"

The man spoke up. "Some. We have to have our stuff freighted in from so far that we can't sell things at a decent price. But we're cheaper than Jules."

"He holds up everybody who comes into his place," the girl added. "I'm not sure he stops at that."

"Mary!" the man said sharply.

"All right, Pa," the girl said. "But I didn't say half as much as some people do."

An awkward silence fell over the store as dusk thickened the shadows. Quint had clutched at the hope that this girl might be Gilda Ryan. But the man had called her Mary. He would have to look elsewhere for Gilda.

"Do you happen to know a girl named Gilda Ryan?" he asked finally, breaking the silence.

But the silence settled down again thicker

than ever, and an uncomfortable prickle began working up Quint's spine.

"You really are new here, ain't you?" the man said finally. "Everybody in Julesburg knows Gilda."

FIVE

Quint let the silence drag out after the man had given his indirect opinion of Gilda Ryan. At least Quint knew that Gilda was in town. But she obviously didn't belong to the same social circle as the people who ran this store.

"Where can I find her?" he asked finally.

"At the saloon across the street this evening, I reckon," the man said, "if you're looking for that kind of company."

"I have to look her up for a friend," Quint said.

"She stays at the boarding house," the girl volunteered.

"Thanks," Quint said. "I'll find her and deliver my message."

He knew from the man's look that any man carrying a message for Gilda Ryan was, to him, of questionable character.

Quint went outside, glancing up at the sign over the door. It was growing dark, but he made out the name, Lem Baxter, Prop., under the General Merchandise sign. The girl was probably his daughter. Mary Baxter was a pretty name, he thought. But perhaps it was a case of the girl making the name seem pretty.

He pushed thoughts of Mary Baxter out of his mind. He had far more important business tonight. Once he found Gilda Ryan he would know whether there was anything in Julesburg worth staying for. If not, he would shake the dust of this town. Jules Beni would be furious if he quit, but Quint had the feeling that Jules was mad at the world most of the time, anyway. He was not the kind of boss Quint would have picked to work for, had he a choice.

At the boarding house, he went into the kitchen to talk to Mrs. Ketrick. If he could catch Gilda Ryan before she went to work, his job would be much simpler. It would take only a minute to knock the heel off his boot and get the note.

"Get out of my kitchen!" Mrs. Ketrick exploded when she saw him. "This isn't the parlor."

"I wanted to ask you something," Quint said. "Is Gilda Ryan here now?"

Mrs. Ketrick drew up her thin shoulders and glared at Quint. "No, she isn't. She ate early and went on to the dance hall. There's a wagon train camped out yonder, and they're expecting a lot of business tonight."

Quint nodded. "I know."

"You'll just have to get in line if you want to see Gilda."

Quint knew what she meant by that, too, but he ignored it. He intended to see Gilda tonight and put his half note with hers. Then, whether anything came of it or not, he would have fulfilled his promise to Joe Linzy.

As soon as supper was over, Quint went out into the street again. There was a different air about the town now. Julesburg was not exactly a town throbbing with night life. But it was alive just the same. Quint guessed a few of the younger single men from the wagon train had come into town. And there were others who lived through the day just to enjoy the life that began with the setting sun.

Quint headed down the street, driven by a single purpose. There were several horses tied in front of the saloon and dance hall. Quint went inside. A row of bracket lamps were burning along one wall, sending light over the room from reflectors behind them. Two big lamps were swinging from the ceiling.

Quint sat at a table close to the door and looked the place over. He half expected to see Cole Fray and his partner, Russ Spark. He had seen them ride out of town this morning, but if Fray was expecting Quint to come to Julesburg looking for Joe Linzy's girl, as Quint suspected, he would not give up his vigil this soon.

He ignored the bar along the one side that stretched almost the full length of the room and concentrated on the open area where the girls were coaxing the men to dance before buying them drinks.

There were five girls out there now, and Quint tried to guess which one was Gilda Ryan. He could not afford to make a mistake about her. All wore dresses of gaudy material with short skirts and had on enough paint and powder to have done credit to Indians on the warpath.

Before Quint had satisfied himself that he knew none of the men at the tables or the bar, one of the girls spotted him alone and approached his table.

"No fun sitting in a corner by yourself," she said invitingly. "Let's have a drink and dance."

"I'm not exactly looking for fun," Quint said. "I'm looking for Gilda Ryan."

The girl's eyes half closed as she leaned forward. "What do you want with Gilda?"

Quint studied the girl before answering. She was tall and sufficiently plump in the right places to be attractive to some men. Her eyes and hair were both as black as an Indian's. Her dress was bright yellow, contrasting sharply with her deeply tanned skin.

"I have a message for her," Quint said. "From Joe Linzy."

The black eyes flew open and the girl caught her breath. "What message?"

"I'll tell it to Gilda," Quint said.

"You're telling it to Gilda now," the girl said. "What's the message?"

"I have something to give to you," Quint said.

Gilda flashed her black eyes over the crowd.

One man was coming across the floor toward them, his steps already a little unsteady.

"Don't give me anything here," she whispered. "Is Joe all right?"

"He's dead," Quint said. "He gave me this message as he was dying."

Her face paled, but she gave no other sign of emotion. "I'll be through here at midnight," she whispered as the man got closer. "Meet me outside and walk me to the boarding house."

Quint nodded as the man staggered up to claim Gilda for a dance. Quint stayed in his chair for a while. He had over three hours to wait. He wished those hours were gone.

After sitting for another half hour and refusing two girls who tried to draw him out on the dance floor or over to the bar, Quint got up and went outside. Just watching Gilda at her work made him wonder again at his evaluation of his short-time partner, Joe Linzy. What kind of a man had Linzy been? He had been engaged to marry Gilda Ryan, and it was obvious what kind of a girl she was. What about the money that was involved? It wasn't hard-earned cash, Quint was sure of that. Joe Linzy had said that Quint and Gilda were to share it when they found it. Quint wondered what he was letting himself in for.

He went back to the boarding house and waited until after eleven. Then he went outside again and wandered down to the dance hall. Maybe Gilda could get away from work more quickly than she had expected. He was sure she would come out as soon as she could. She must be eager to get the message from Joe Linzy.

Most of the horses were gone from the hitch-rack in front of the saloon when Quint went back down the street. All other lights in town had gone out. The quiet of the night was ruffled only by the noise of the music and laughter from the saloon.

Quint stopped at the corner of the building, wishing now that he had waited until the appointed hour of midnight. An uneasiness for which he could find no cause trickled through him. He considered going inside and waiting there for Gilda to finish her evening's work. But maybe she would not want those in the saloon to see her walking out with him.

Finally, after two more men came out and staggered up the street, Quint did move toward the door. But he didn't reach it. A man stepped out from a spot where he had apparently been watching those who came and went. The light was dim here, but Quint got a good enough look to recognize Cole Fray, the man who had killed Joe Linzy. He had come back as Quint had suspected he might.

"No fuss, friend," Fray said softly. "Just step around the corner where we can talk."

"We've got nothing to talk about," Quint said, standing still.

But the instant he said it, he realized he had made a mistake. He felt the cold prod of something in his back.

"Shall I let him have it, Cole?" a voice behind Quint said.

"No, you fool!" Fray snapped. "We don't want the whole town on us. Anyway, we just want to visit with him. Come on."

This time Quint obeyed. He had quickly evaluated the impatience in the voice of the man with the gun. Despite Fray's orders, the man would gladly shoot Quint at the least excuse. Quint was certain of that.

He allowed himself to be guided around the corner of the saloon into the darkness that swallowed up everything but the feel of the two men.

"Now then," Fray said softly. "Hand over that note that Linzy gave you and everything will be all right."

"What note?" Quint said.

Fray's voice hardened like hot iron dipped in water. "Joe Linzy told me he had given you the paper that told where the money is. That money doesn't belong to you. You did nothing to get it. But you'll die for it if you don't hand it over."

"I don't know anything about any money," Quint said. "I only knew Joe Linzy a month."

"That was long enough for him to trust you with that note. He told me that when he knew he didn't have long to live. He wouldn't lie at a time like that."

"Maybe you didn't know Linzy as well as you thought," Quint said.

He considered trying to reach for his gun and fight it out. But every move he made brought a sharp thrust of the gun in his back. He would never get his own gun in his hand before he died.

"You saw what happened to Linzy," Fray said, and Quint could feel the suppressed rage in him. "You can get the same by being stubborn."

Quint said nothing. There was nothing more to say unless he told Fray where the half note was. And even that probably would not save him from the beating. That half note would do Fray no more good than it did Quint. And Fray would be sure that Quint was holding back the other half.

The first blow came suddenly. Quint had expected Fray to try a while longer to make him talk. Fray's fist caught Quint in the stomach and drove him backward. Quint felt the gun prod deep into his back before the man behind him could get out of the way.

With the gun gone from his back, Quint lunged forward, feeling free at last to defend himself. It was too dark for the other man to use the gun, for now both Quint and Fray had changed positions.

Quint drove forward, lashing out at what he felt rather than saw. He got the deep satisfaction of hearing a sharp grunt and a man swear softly. If he could get his hands on Cole Fray, he would kill him. He had promised himself he would kill the man who had beaten Joe Linzy to death. His estimation of his onetime friend, Linzy, had dropped considerably, but his resolution to deal with his killer had not faded.

Quint had to battle two assailants but he had one advantage over them. Whenever he contacted a man, he knew it was an enemy.

He backed away as he heard the two men in front of him. He didn't dare let them get him between them. When one man threw a punch, Quint struck back. Quint took a fist on the side of his face, then thought he landed a blow just as punishing.

Then both men charged him at the same time. Somehow they had gotten coordinated; each knew where the other was. Quint met the charge, striking out with all the force he had, then falling back quickly. He was fighting for his life now, and he knew it. They had killed one man because he hadn't turned over the half note. They wouldn't hesitate to kill another. But turning over the half note would not save him, Quint knew; nor would it have saved Joe Linzy.

Quint backed against the wall where he fought off the two men, grimly satisfied to hand out as much punishment as he was absorbing.

But then a hard fist caught him on the side of the jaw and rocked his head back against the wall.

The darkness filled with tiny spears of light, and he saw things that no man should see in the dark. His guard dropped momentarily, and another fist crashed against his face.

He heard a triumphant oath, and he realized that the men's eyes had grown used to the darkness, that they could see a little. But his own vision was blurred by more than darkness. He knew that in seconds he would see nothing unless he could wiggle out of this trap.

He tried to duck away, but a hard fist, or maybe the barrel of a gun, chopped down against the back of his head. He felt himself falling to the ground, but he didn't feel himself hit it.

SIX

Regaining consciousness, Quint was not sure whether he was alive or dead. The bright flashes in front of his eyes belonged to no world he had ever known.

But then the flashes started to subside, and he began thinking straight. His thoughts went to the note crammed inside the heel of his boot. He felt them; both heels were in place. But his pockets were turned wrong side out. Fray and his companion had done a thorough job of searching him.

The town was dark. Even the lights in the saloon had disappeared. Quint had no idea how long he had been unconscious. He staggered to his feet, leaning against the building. He saw that he had been dragged to the back of the saloon. He was amazed that he was still alive. And he still had the half note. Surely Fray must be convinced now that he didn't have the note at all.

But Quint knew that was foolish reasoning. Cole Fray would never give up until he found the money that Joe Linzy had hidden. Moreover, Linzy had told Fray that Quint possessed the note. Quint wondered how safe Gilda Ryan was. Surely Fray knew about her, too, since he knew so much about Linzy and his business. If Quint let her see this half note so that she knew where the money was, he might be delivering her death warrant.

Quint leaned against the wall of the saloon until he felt capable of walking. Then he made his way slowly to the boarding house and up to his room. He found the door of his room already open, and it was no surprise to him, when he lit the lamp, to see his room literally torn to pieces. Fray had done a thorough job of searching for the note. But he had failed. Quint got some solace in imagining Fray's consternation.

Quint found it hard to get up when Mrs. Ketrick shrieked that breakfast was ready. He considered staying where he was. But he had to eat. And the only way he was going to be able to eat was to work—at least until he and Gilda got together and found that money. If he failed to show up on time at the station, he knew that Jules would fire him. He was sure that Jules would like nothing better than to kick a man when he was down. And Quint was about as near down and out this morning as he had ever been.

He staggered down to breakfast, ignoring the inquiring looks cast his way. He wondered if he might not find Cole Fray and his partner, Russ Spark, at the breakfast table. There was no other place in town to stay, but they were missing.

So was Gilda Ryan, and Quint had hoped to find an opportunity to talk to her. But he realized, when he thought of it, that Gilda probably had her breakfast about noon.

Jules scowled at Quint when he reported for work but said nothing. Quint had the feeling that, as long as he did the two men's work that Jules had assigned him, Jules wouldn't squawk. But he would demand the full measure of work he expected from him.

The only one to show any real concern for Quint's condition was the old man who worked with the horses, Mike Shield. Mike suggested that Quint lie down in the hay at the back of the stable and rest a while when he came out to help get the stage horses ready. Quint was tempted, but he refused.

"You got to take care of yourself around Jules," Mike warned Quint softly as they watched the stage pull out after dinner. "He'll work you any way he can."

Quint had the feeling that Mike meant to put more than one meaning to his words. Quint respected Mike's warning. Mike had known Jules for quite a while. He had been working for him ever since the stage line had switched its route from Smoky Hill up to the Platte a year ago. It didn't take that long, Quint guessed, to learn the kind of man Jules Beni was.

Quint got through the day and returned to the boarding house where he flopped into bed, not even bothering with supper. He wanted to see

Gilda, but that would have to wait. He might run into another fight with Fray and Spark if he went up to the saloon tonight. And he knew he could not survive another battle like the previous one. Morning found him stiff and sore, but feeling something like a man again.

Each day he expected to see Fray or Spark around the station, but the days passed and they didn't appear. Quint was satisfied. He hoped he never saw them again unless he had a gun in his hand. On those terms, he would like to meet Fray.

A few nights after his beating, Quint felt up to making an attempt to see Gilda Ryan again. He had waited, thinking that she would contact him. He had told her he had a message from Joe Linzy, and she had seemed very excited about it. But she had not even spoken to him since that night; in fact, she seemed to be avoiding him.

He checked his gun carefully before venturing out into the dark street. Tonight, if Cole Fray jumped him, there would be a gun battle, not a fist fight. The day would surely come when they would meet, and Quint had to be ready. The pale-eyed gunman would never rest until he got his hands on that money, and Quint doubted if he could do that until he assembled the two parts of the note Linzy had written.

As was usual after dark, the street was almost deserted. Only a few brave men tried to run cattle in this country, for it was, in effect, still Indian country. So the night life of this town had to come from the people in town and any wagon train camped close by.

Quint walked down to the saloon, peering in cautiously before stepping through the doors. But neither Fray nor his partner, Spark, was there.

Quint sat at the same table as before and watched the girls maneuvering around the room. He caught Gilda's eye and motioned for her to come over. But she sent another girl instead.

Quint frowned and told the girl he wasn't thirsty and didn't want to dance. It was obvious that Gilda was avoiding him. He couldn't understand that, not when he had this note from Linzy.

Quint got up and moved around where he could intercept Gilda, but she neatly avoided him. Quint was stymied. But this was no place to create a scene, not when the cause of it had to be kept secret. So he went back outside, determined to talk to her at the boarding house away from curious ears.

But Quint found that Gilda was also adept at avoiding him there. She ate breakfast about eleven o'clock, he learned from Mrs. Ketrick. Lately, she had been eating an early supper and going up to the saloon before Quint got off work.

Quint considered slipping away from the station at an hour when he could catch Gilda at the boarding house. But with Jules eyeing him constantly, that wouldn't be easy.

Then one day, just after the eastbound stage had pulled out, Jules slapped on his hat and went to the door.

"I've got an errand to do," he said. "You watch the station. Nothing much to do now, anyway."

Quint nodded. He had never seen Jules in such a hurry. He was usually rather slow in his movements. He watched him get his horse and ride off to the south. Quint wondered what errand Jules could have off there in the broken hills south of the river.

But he turned his thoughts back to his own problems. It wouldn't be long before Gilda would come out of her room at the boarding house, eat supper, then go on up to the saloon. As Jules had said, there was little to do around the station now. The pony-express rider had already galloped off, and the last stage of the day had gone on to the east, carrying passengers and a load of gold from the Cherry Creek diggings.

As usual, Mike Shield came in from the stable after the last stage had departed.

"Think you could watch the station for me for a few minutes?" Quint asked. "I've got to go over to the boarding house."

"Sure," Mike said. "Ain't nothing to do here unless some freighter drops in."

Quint waited until he was sure that Gilda would be eating her supper, then he left Mike in charge of the station and went over to the boarding house. He didn't go inside. He didn't want Martha Ketrick to hear what might be said. He felt she would be a terrible gossip if she could find someone to tell her stories to.

Quint was waiting at the side of the building when Gilda came out. She glanced apprehensively at the stage station, then turned toward the saloon, walking rapidly. Quint stepped out from the corner of the building to intercept her. She stopped with a gasp, and Quint thought she was going to turn and run back inside.

"How come I'm poison to you all of a sudden?" Quint demanded.

"Nobody said you were."

"You've been acting like it. You seemed anxious enough to see me the first night I got here."

"You didn't meet me that night."

"I got waylaid. You surely could see that from the way I looked the next day."

"Did you lose your message from Joe Linzy?"

Quint shook his head. "No. I've still got it."

"You'll never get my half," Gilda said and dodged around him, running toward the saloon.

Quint let her go. He knew now why she was so afraid of him. Somehow she had gotten the idea that he was trying to get her half of the note for himself instead of delivering his half to her. That made a ticklish situation. Gilda Ryan was evidently a suspicious person, the kind who trusted no one, dangerous. She would be determined now to get the half note that he had. And she would try to get it without risking the loss of her own, which meant she could be as dangerous to Quint as Cole Fray.

Quint returned to the station and was working when Jules arrived. Jules said nothing, but carried his saddlebags to the rear of the station before coming back to work. When Mike came in promptly at quitting time, he was shaking his head. Quint asked him what was wrong.

"Take a look at the horse Jules rode," Mike said softly. "I know he's a big man. But he must have ridden like the Indians were chasing him to wear a horse out like that."

Quint didn't look at the horse. Jules was watching them with suspicious eyes. If Quint was guessing right, he had reason to.

The next day, word spread that the eastbound stage had been held up the afternoon before at Devil's Dive, about five miles east of the Julesburg station and that the gold shipment had been taken. Nothing much was said about it around the station. This wasn't the first gold shipment that had been lost at Devil's Dive. Quint tried to remember if Jules had been away when the other robberies had taken place. Now that he thought about it, he was sure that he had been. But that was none of Quint's business. His worry still hinged on that note he had hidden in the heel of his boot. Sooner or later, either Cole Fray or Gilda would try to get it. And it was easier to search a dead man than a live one.

Lem Baxter came up to the station that afternoon. Quint was surprised. Baxter's store was running competition to Jules' station; they had little business with each other.

"Mary and I would like for you to come over for supper tonight," Lem said.

Quint's spirits rose. He had been dropping in at the store quite often after work, though he seldom bought anything. He had not known Mary long, but it was long enough to fill any idle moments with wild dreams.

"I'll be there," he said.

He was still puzzled by the invitation when he went to the Baxters' living quarters in the rear of the store that evening. It was not long before he suspected that the invitation had not been prompted entirely by a desire to be sociable.

"What are they saying about the holdup yesterday at Devil's Dive?" Lem Baxter asked while Mary finished setting the table.

"Wasn't much said about it around the station," Quint said.

"Was Jules gone yesterday afternoon?"

Quint nodded. "He rode out just after the stage left. Got back late with a very tired horse."

"You know where he was, don't you?" Lem pressed.

“I’ve got ideas,” Quint said.

“Don’t you know you’re being linked with Jules?” Mary asked, shoving a kettle to the back of the stove and turning to face Quint. “They say you’re covering up for him there in the station while he goes out and robs the stages.”

“Who says that?” Quint demanded.

“Too many people,” Mary said. “I don’t like it.”

“I didn’t suppose others suspected Jules.”

“Everybody suspects him, I think,” Lem said. “You notice it’s always the stages with the gold or well-heeled passengers that get held up. Jules is the one who is in the best position to know about those stages.”

“Why would they say I’m helping him?” Quint asked.

“Partly because you work for him,” Mary said. “But mostly it’s because of the lies that Jules has been dropping around.”

Quint leaned forward. “What has Jules been telling?”

Lem answered. “I heard him say in the saloon the other night that you had a habit of disappearing just before these robberies take place.”

“You’d better quit that job while you can,” Mary said.

“That wouldn’t help,” Lem said. “Not now. If there is another robbery, Jules would still say it was Dan who did it. If Dan left town, Jules would just say that he was holed up out in the hills and robbing the stages from there."

"I'll settle with Jules," Quint said, his anger growing as he thought about it.

"Just sit tight for a while," Lem advised. "It will take more than Jules to convict you. His reputation doesn't smell like roses."

Quint felt there was more behind Lem's advice than he was expressing. But he had to admit it was wise counsel. He would gain nothing but a fight if he braced Jules. He would lose his job and maybe much more. He could not afford to get in trouble with the law. The only law that could touch him now was the law of the Leavenworth and Pike's Peak Express Company. But that would be enough to drag him back where the law of eastern Kansas could grab him for shooting Sam Jardine. He didn't dare let that happen.

For the next few days, Jules was his usual surly self, saying little except to give orders and keep up the barrier that barred everyone from his personal life.

Then a letter came to Jules on the stage from the east. It looked official, and Jules scowled when he looked at it. Unable to read it, he finally had Quint read it to him. It was from Ben Ficklin, superintendent of the Leavenworth and Pike's Peak Express Company. Its short, terse sentences informed Jules that he was being removed from his position as agent at the Julesburg station.

Quint thought Jules would explode when he heard the letter. He swore lustily in a language Quint didn't understand; Quint, however, had no trouble comprehending that Jules was using every vile term he knew.

"They think I'm robbing those stages," he finally shouted. "Well, I'll straighten them out on that. You're the one who's doing that!" He pointed a finger at Quint. "I'll prove it."

"That's a lie and you know it," Quint shot back.

"You can't call me a liar!" Jules screamed. "They'll find a dead stage robber when they get here."

Quint knew Jules' intentions then. If he could produce a dead man that he swore was the robber, they might accept his story. Quint didn't think they would, but Jules did. And what Jules thought was going to dictate what he did the next few minutes.

Jules was going to try to kill Quint. And Quint wasn't sure that he couldn't do it.

SEVEN

Quint wished he had his gun. But he had hung it with his hat when he came to work. Jules wasn't wearing a gun either. But Quint doubted if he would choose to fight with a gun, anyway.

Jules moved toward Quint like a big bear, his arms swinging out from his huge body. Quint held his ground, watching for any quick move on Jules' part. He had to stay out of the grasp of those powerful arms. They could crush the life out of a man, and Quint was sure that was Jules' intention.

Jules suddenly lunged toward Quint, but Quint stepped to one side, hammering a hard fist to Jules' head as he went past. Jules only shook his head and turned to charge again. Quint backed away, stepping quickly out of Jules' reach at the last instant. Jules turned like a disgruntled bull and charged at Quint again. Quint had the feeling that Jules would keep this up until he had worn him down enough to catch him.

But the pattern changed suddenly when Quint's foot caught in some rope on the floor as he was twisting away from Jules. He fell heavily as he tried to untangle his feet, and Jules pounced on him and wrapped his arms around his body. Quint fought desperately, pounding his fists into Jules' face, bringing the blood in a spurt from his nose.

But he knew he couldn't conquer him this way. Jules was tightening his arms, ignoring the punishment Quint was handing him, confident that he could win against anything Quint could do as long as he kept his arms locked around him.

Quint brought up a knee and got it wedged against Jules' big body. Pushing with all his remaining strength, he shoved the big man backward. Quint rolled over and struggled to his feet, knowing that he had to keep away from Jules; he couldn't break a hold like that again.

But Jules was standing still now. Mike Shield was in the doorway, holding a shotgun on him.

"Just lay off," Mike said. "I don't know what the fuss is about. But I'm taking sides, anyway."

"I'll kill you both for this!" Jules hissed.

"Not now you won't," Mike said. "Come on, Dan. Let's go home. 'Pears that our work is done for today."

Quint got his hat and gun, feeling confident again as he faced Jules.

"He'll be cooled off tomorrow," Mike said as they left the station. "He flares up easy and he cools off easy. Coming back to work, are you?"

"According to that letter I read to him," Quint said, "tomorrow is the day they're bringing a replacement for Jules as agent here. I think I'll be here when they come."

"Hope I can keep my job," Mike said. "It's the

only job around here I can do. Maybe a new man will be decent to work for."

Jules only scowled at Quint when he came to the station the next day. Quint watched for a sneak attack, but apparently Jules had something more important on his mind than beating Quint to a pulp.

When the stage from the east rolled in, Quint helped Mike unhitch the horses. He saw two men get out of the coach and enter the station. Quint, dismissed by a nod from Mike, headed for the station.

He arrived at the door in time to hear Jules shout something at a man named Ficklin. That would be Ben Ficklin, the superintendent of the line. The other man was rather tall and solidly built with brown hair and penetrating eyes.

"This is Jack Slade," Ficklin said. "He's taking over as agent for this station. Not only that, Mr. Beni, investigation has proved that you have appropriated a lot of items that belong to the Leavenworth and Pike's Peak Express Company. You will be required to return these items or reimburse the company for their loss."

Jules swore. Then, seeing Quint in the doorway, he jabbed a finger at him. "There's your crook, Ficklin. There's the man who's been stealing your stuff and robbing the stages."

"Who's he?" Ficklin asked, looking at Quint.

"I'm Dan Quint," Quint said before Jules

could say anything more. “I’ve been working at the station for quite a while. But I haven’t taken anything or robbed any stages.”

“Can you prove it?” Slade asked.

“He doesn’t need to,” Ficklin said. “I have all the proof I need, and it all points directly at Jules Beni. Are you willing to reimburse the company for what it has lost, Mr. Beni?”

Jules tried to yell something, but all that came out was a string of stuttered words that Quint couldn’t understand. Quint glanced at Ficklin. He had never seen a man that looked more like a solid rock. And Slade, standing beside him, only added to the picture of strength. Quint had heard stories of Jack Slade, who already had a reputation for being a tough man, very good with the gun he wore low on his hip. It was evident to Quint as he looked at Jules that the station agent had also heard of Slade.

Finally, Jules’ words became coherent. “What about my trading post here? I own that.”

“The company will buy your stock. If you compensate for the list of items you have taken, you’ll be free to go your way. Otherwise, the company will prosecute.”

Jules sputtered for a moment, glaring at the two men. Then he seemed to wilt. “All right. I pay. You buy my trading post.”

Quint watched the transaction. Jules swore steadily as he was presented with a list of losses the stage company had attributed to Jules' thievery. Quint guessed from the willingness with which Jules paid up that the company's list was not nearly complete. Jules probably was making a good profit on the deal in addition to being let go scot free.

When Jules and the superintendent of the express line had completed their business, Ficklin turned to Quint.

"According to our report, Mr. Quint, you have had nothing to do with Jules' stealing."

"I just worked for him," Quint said.

"You want to keep on working here?"

"I'd like to."

Ficklin turned to Slade. "How about it, Jack? You want to keep him?"

Slade nodded. "Why not? I need somebody here who knows more about the business than I do. I'll catch on fast enough. If he tries anything funny, we'll have a funeral and I'll get a new man."

Ficklin turned back to Quint. "Looks like you're hired."

Quint wasn't sure how well he would like Jack Slade. He would be a tough boss, he decided. But he still had his job, and that was important to him now.

Quint had one conviction that he didn't believe either Ficklin or Slade shared with him. They seemed to think that they were through with

Jules when they settled with him and he walked out. Quint knew Jules better than that. Jules could store up an enormous quantity of hate in his heart. And he was taking a lot of it with him as he left. He would strike back in some way sometime; Quint was sure of it. And when he did, somebody would die.

For the next two days, Quint spent most of his time acquainting Jack Slade with the workings of the Julesburg station. Slade could be a rough taskmaster, Quint decided, but he seemed to be fair. That was more than he could say for Jules Beni.

Quint's anger smoldered as he remembered how Jules had tried to shove the blame for the robberies off on him. Jules must have felt he could blame a drifter for the robberies and make the charge stick. But the attempt had failed. That would put Quint on Jules' blacklist, too. Quint felt that he knew Jules well enough now to know how he reasoned things out. And since he had failed, he would hold Quint responsible, just as he would hold Jack Slade responsible for replacing him. Both Quint and Slade would have reason to be on the alert until they knew for sure that Jules Beni had left the country. Quint didn't think he would go.

As soon as Quint got his half note together with Gilda Ryan's, he would determine whether there was anything to hold him in Julesburg. If not, he could move on to Denver. As long as he had the note in his possession, he was facing the certainty that, sooner or later, Cole Fray or Gilda Ryan would try again to get it from him, either by force or trickery. Now he was faced with added danger from Jules. If he got rid of the note and went on to Denver, he would be free of all these troubles.

Jack Slade caught on to the workings of the station quickly, and Quint felt that his pledge to show Slade the ropes had been fulfilled. But the other half of his plan, solving the mystery of the note, was no nearer completion. Then Mike Shield came into the station just at closing time one evening to call Quint off to one side.

"Gilda just stopped by the barn," Mike reported. "She left a message for you?"

Suspicion tugged at Quint. "What does she want?"

"Nothing for herself," Mike said. "There's a train camped out south. She was out drumming up business for the dance hall. She said there was somebody in the train inquiring for you."

Quint frowned. "Who?"

"She didn't say. She seemed anxious to get away, as if she thought she was in danger while she was here."

Quint nodded. Evidently, she still thought he planned to steal her half of the note. But he dismissed that worry. Who in the train would be inquiring after him? The law from eastern Kansas? Or maybe Judd Hurley himself? If it was Judd, Quint wanted to see him. He had a score to settle with him.

"Got a horse I can borrow?" Quint asked.

"Got one already saddled for you," Mike said. "Better be careful. No telling what might be waiting for you."

Quint nodded. It could be an accomplice of Gilda's. This might be her plan to get Quint's note without showing her own.

Quint checked his gun and rode out south of the station to the big area where the wagon trains usually camped. He rode cautiously, one hand on the butt of his gun, as he came inside the circle of wagons. He looked for the wagon master, but before he saw him, he heard his name called. His fingers involuntarily tightened on the butt of his gun, but then they pulled away as if the handle were hot.

"Dan! Dan!"

Quint wheeled. "Ma! I didn't expect . . ."

He swung off his horse to receive his mother's embrace. Then he pushed her back.

"What are you doing on this train, Ma? Is Judd along?"

Ann Hurley shook her head. "Judd didn't come. I—I left him, Dan. After you had that fight with Sam Jardine, Judd got so poison-mean, I couldn't stand it any longer. He seemed to think the law would catch you and hang you for Sam's killing. When it didn't, the stories began going around that Judd had tricked you into fighting Sam. Judd got so mean that a saint couldn't have lived with him."

Quint nodded. "I can believe that. He didn't have to change much. Where are you heading?"

"I started to California eight years ago with your father," she said. "I decided I'd go there now. I thought you might have gone there instead of Denver. I've been inquiring for you at every station just in case you had stopped somewhere."

"You'd better stay here in Julesburg with me," Quint said. "I'm working for the agent at the stage station here."

"I don't have much money. Judd tried to keep it all but I did slip out some. Could I find work here?"

"Maybe," Quint said, although he had doubts about that. "But I'm not much of a man if I can't earn a living for the two of us. Get your things and tell the wagon boss you're staying here."

When she had told the wagon master that she was leaving the train and Quint had made arrangements to get her belongings, Quint asked her about the situation back at the farm.

"Is the law there still after me?"

"The sheriff isn't out combing the brush for you, if that's what you mean," Ann Hurley said. "But he'd still like to talk to you."

"To hang me for killing Sam Jardine, I suppose," Quint said.

"No. People are convinced now that you were pushed into that fight. An inquiry has already been made. It was declared a fair fight—that Sam reached for his gun before you did. So you're no longer charged with murder."

"Then why are they looking for me?"

"They want you for a witness, Dan. It's Judd who is in trouble now. You know that Sam Jardine was robbed the week before you had that fight with him. His knife was stolen in the robbery. People have decided that Judd robbed Sam, then planted that knife by your horse to make you go after Sam."

"I did just what Judd wanted me to," Quint said disgustedly. "I figured that all out the next day, after I ran away."

"They asked me if I had seen Judd with that knife, but I didn't dare say I had," Ann said. "Blix, of course, denied that Judd ever had the knife. But they think you must have seen him with it, even though you might not have paid much attention to it at the time."

Quint nodded. "I did, all right, but I didn't make the connection until it was too late."

"Your testimony along with the evidence they already have will be enough to convict Judd of robbing Sam and of pushing you into that fight." She put a hand on Quint's arm. "Dan, you've got to be careful. Don't let Judd find you. He'll kill you if he gets half a chance."

"What makes you think he'll ever find me out here?"

"He'll come west," Ann said positively. "He's staying there now just to sell the property. He's so greedy he wants every penny he can get. But he won't stay long. He knows that if the sheriff uncovers any positive proof that he robbed Sam, he'll slap him in jail. Judd aims to get out of the country before that happens. But he also knows that if you ever testify against him, he'll be caught and thrown in prison. So he'll try to kill you if he ever finds you."

"Judd can't sell the farm," Quint said.

"No," Ann agreed. "That's in your name. But he'll sell everything on it."

Quint took his mother to the boarding house and got her a room. The news that she had brought of his fight with Sam Jardine back home was encouraging. But now that the accusing finger of the law was pointing at Judd Hurley, he would be even more desperate to see Quint dead. The posse hadn't caught him, even after Judd had made sure that Quint was afoot; Cole Fray hadn't killed him as he had been hired to do. Quint wondered if Judd wouldn't assume the responsibility of doing it himself now.

Quint felt sure that Judd would come looking for him as soon as he sold off the things on the farm. Like Quint's mother, Judd would probably inquire at every station along the way. He would want to eliminate Quint so that he could not testify against him.

Quint was not going to dodge a clash with Judd. In fact, he was going to watch the passing trains for Judd. Judd would have money gotten from what he had sold from the farm. That money belonged to Quint's mother. She had bought the farm with money left her by Quint's father, and he was sure she had bought everything on the farm, too. Judd Hurley had never made much money for himself.

Quint decided he liked to work for Slade much better than he had for Jules, especially when his wages were raised. Now he had no trouble making ends meet, even with the added expense of keeping his mother. Slade and his wife, Virginia, moved into a house close by the trading post.

Rumors started trickling back to the station that Jules had not left the country but was just waiting for an opportunity to get even with Slade, whom he blamed for most of his troubles.

"What do you make of all this talk?" Slade asked Quint one afternoon after a man had come by, saying he had seen Jules and heard him making threats against Slade.

"I'd keep my eyes open if I were you," Quint said. "Jules is a mean man."

Slade laughed. “I’m no angel myself.”

Quint checked every wagon train that came by. He found the one he was looking for much sooner than he expected.

He rode out as usual after work one evening to inspect a train that had pulled in and camped late in the afternoon. He found the wagon master and stopped to chat with him.

“Where are you from?” he asked.

“Started from Westport Landing,” the wagon boss said. “Picked up three more wagons from St. Joe as we came up the road.”

Quint’s interest quickened. “Is there a man named Judd Hurley in one of the wagons from St. Joe?”

The wagon master’s eyebrows raised. “As a matter of fact, there is. Him and his son. I believe his name is Blix.”

Quint nodded, going tight inside. “Which wagon?”

The wagon master pointed. “Down in that end of camp. I can’t tell from here exactly which wagon.”

“I’ll find them,” Quint said, and started across camp, leading his horse. The time had come for his showdown with Judd. Anticipation and caution warred within him, leaving him cold inside.

EIGHT

Quint caught a glimpse of Blix first, ducking around a corner of a wagon. He was sure that Blix had seen him. A moment later, Judd's head appeared around the corner of the wagon, but ducked back immediately.

Quint dropped the reins of his horse and broke into a run, heading directly for the wagon. He reached the back of the wagon just as Judd Hurley was climbing out, a gun in his hand. When Judd looked up, he was staring into the bore of Quint's gun.

"Figuring on using that gun, Judd?" Quint asked.

Judd's mouth dropped open. "No, of course not," he said finally. "I just like to have my gun handy."

"Drop it, Judd!"

Judd let the gun slip from his fingers. "You figuring on murdering me?"

"All I figure on doing is collecting the money that belongs to Ma."

Judd scowled darkly. "I don't owe her nothing. She ran out on me."

"She said you stayed on the farm to sell everything there. Whose money bought that stuff?"

"Her money was my money when we got married," Judd said sullenly.

"You're going to have to convince me of that," Quint said grimly.

In his concentration on Judd, Quint had forgotten Blix for the moment. Now he felt a jab in his back and he regretted his carelessness.

"Drop that gun, Dan!" Blix snapped.

Quint started to relax his grip on his gun and Judd stepped forward to grab it.

"Good work, Blix. He was going to kill me."

As Judd yanked the gun from Quint's hands, Quint lunged forward, grabbing Judd and jerking him around between him and Blix. Blix swore, but he didn't shoot.

Judd fought back, dropping the gun he had just jerked from Quint. Quint let himself be thrown to the ground but he hit it rolling, pulling Judd with him. They rolled away from the wagon into the circle of the camp. Men came running from all sides. Blix danced around, trying to get a clean shot at Quint, but Quint managed to keep Judd on top often enough that Blix didn't dare shoot.

Judd was pounding Quint with his fists and Quint was getting in a few blows of his own. But most of his effort was concentrated on keeping Judd between him and Blix.

"What's going on?" a voice yelled above the noise.

"He's trying to kill Pa," Blix yelled.

"Give me that gun!" the commanding voice shouted. "Stop the fight!"

Quint was aware that Blix's gun had been jerked from his hand, but nobody stepped in to stop Quint's fight with Judd. Quint concentrated on punishing Judd now. But he had barely started swinging his fists when Judd pulled a knife from his boot top.

Quint darted forward, catching Judd's wrist. A gasp went up from the men nearby when they saw the knife. Quint rolled suddenly and jerked Judd over him, holding the knife away from him. Judd screamed as he landed on the knife.

Quint rolled away from Judd, hearing Blix yell wildly, "He knifed Pa!"

As Quint scrambled to his feet, he saw Judd lunge up. The knife had slashed through his clothes over the ribs, but from the way Judd was moving, Quint was sure that it had not cut through the ribs. It would make a bloody, painful wound, but not a fatal one.

Judd wheeled toward the wagon and Quint started after him, but the wagon master caught his arm.

"Get your gun and get out of here!" he snapped. "I don't know what your quarrel is with Hurley. But it's finished right now."

Quint glanced around the ring of faces. If he argued the point with the wagon boss, he would be fighting every man in that circle.

"He stole some money that belonged to my mother," Quint said.

"I'll talk to him," the wagon boss said. "You come back in the morning when things have quieted down, and we'll settle this."

It wasn't what Quint wanted, but he could do nothing more now. He was sure that the wagon master wouldn't learn anything in Quint's favor when he talked to Judd.

"I'll be back in the morning," Quint said, and he picked up his gun where Judd had dropped it.

He mounted his horse and rode toward town, feeling the naked hatred in Blix's stare as he passed him. Judd had disappeared inside a wagon.

Quint slipped into his room at the boarding house and cleaned up before his mother could see him. He said nothing about Judd being in the train camped outside town. He wondered if he should tell her and decided to wait until he checked with the wagon boss the next morning.

Quint was at the wagon camp the next morning before sunup. The camp was stirring, getting ready to move out. Quint found the wagon master.

"What did Judd tell you?" he asked.

"He didn't tell me anything," the wagon boss said. "After I got the men back to their own wagons, I went looking for Hurley, but he had disappeared. So had his boy, Blix. They weren't in camp last night, and they're not here this morning either. You didn't knife him bad enough that he might have crawled off and died, did you?"

"I didn't knife him at all," Quint said testily. "It was his knife, and he was trying to stab me with it. But I don't think he was hurt bad, the way he got up and ran. And I didn't lay a finger on Blix. He certainly didn't crawl off and die."

The man shook his head. "No, of course not. Maybe they just decided to stop off here at Julesburg."

"I reckon that's it," Quint said, frowning as he considered what this meant.

The only reason Judd and Blix would have for stopping at Julesburg would be to kill Quint. With Quint dead, Judd Hurley would be freed of the worry that Quint might someday go back east with the testimony that would put Hurley behind bars.

Besides that, if Quint was dead, Judd could probably find some way to get clear title to that farm back on the Missouri River. He wouldn't live on the farm, but he could sell it and live well off the money. Judd Hurley had everything to gain and nothing to lose by stopping off in Julesburg and waiting for his chance to kill Quint.

Three days after the wagon train moved on, Quint caught a glimpse of Blix Hurley in front of Lem Baxter's store. By the time he got there, however, Blix was gone. But seeing Blix eliminated any doubt he had whether Judd and

Blix were staying somewhere close to Julesburg, waiting for a chance to kill him.

More reports came into the stage station from drivers who had seen Jules Beni out on the trail. He was still breathing threats against Slade. Jules wasn't blaming his troubles on the line superintendent, Ben Ficklin, who had fired him, but was concentrating all his fury on Jack Slade, who had taken his job.

Two stages were held up and the gold shipments taken. Slade was furious. There was no doubt in anybody's mind that Jules Beni had held up those stages, although the drivers couldn't be sure because the bandit had been masked.

"He's stealing from the company worse than ever," Slade stormed. "We've got to stop him."

"Killing him will be the only way you'll stop him," Quint said. "He's a mighty stubborn man."

"If that's the case, we'll kill him," Slade said without hesitation. "I've been given the job of keeping this line free of road agents, and I intend to do it."

Two mornings later, Quint arrived at work to find Mike Shield almost beside himself with excitement. Slade arrived a minute behind Quint and Mike ran to him, waving his arms frantically.

"Somebody stole four horses last night," he shouted.

"You sleep in the stable," Slade exploded. "Didn't you hear the thieves?"

“No,” Mike said. “I didn’t hear a thing out of the ordinary.”

“Indians, maybe,” Slade suggested.

“I doubt it,” Mike said. “The horses would snort and raise Cain at the smell of an Indian.”

“Then who?” Slade demanded.

“It must have been somebody the horses knew,” Quint said. “They would get pretty excited if any stranger came in among them. All of these horses have been here before between stage runs.”

“Jules Beni!” Slade spat the words out like bullets.

Quint nodded. “I was thinking that. We’re pretty sure he’s been robbing the stages. Why wouldn’t he take some horses too?”

“We’re going after those horses, Quint,” Slade said. “They tell me Jules is headquartering at a ranch up the river a ways. Mike, can you run things here for a while?”

“I reckon,” Mike said. “Just so you get back by stage time.”

It wasn’t a long ride up the river to the ranch where Jules Beni was supposed to be staying. When they arrived at the place, it appeared deserted. There were some horses in the corrals, but no men were in sight.

“Better ride in with our eyes open,” Quint suggested.

“A man who doesn’t keep his eyes open will soon be a dead man,” Slade said. “We’ll take a look at the horses first to see if any stage animals are there."

Quint didn't expect to find any stage horses in the corrals. Surely no man, not even a defiant one like Jules Beni, would steal horses, then keep them in a corral for any man to ride up and identify.

They reached the corral without a challenge and dismounted. Slade climbed into the corral and stood looking at the horses as they milled past him.

"Our four horses are here, all right," he reported.

Quint stared at the horses in surprise. "Shall we cut them out and take them home?" he asked finally, wondering what Slade's next move would be.

"I want to know who took them," Slade said. "I'll see if I can find any clues."

Quint waited at the corral while Slade walked toward the house. Still there was no sign of life. Slade reached the door, opened it, then stepped back out on the porch to call to Quint.

"Nobody here, I guess," he said. "Might as well cut out our horses and start them toward town."

Quint yelled a warning as Jules Beni suddenly stepped into the doorway behind Slade, a gun in his hand. As Slade wheeled, Jules fired several times. Slade went down like a polled ox, falling into the yard.

While Quint watched, almost stunned, Jules reached behind him and brought out a shotgun. He pulled the trigger, the pellets hitting Slade's body and making it jerk.

Quint started forward then stopped as Jules swung the shotgun toward him. The range was too great for the shotgun and Quint considered pulling his gun and taking by Slade's fight. But Jules still had his six-gun, and this was a job for the law, anyway. He couldn't help Slade now by buying into the fight.

"Get this horse thief's carcass out of here," Jules yelled at Quint.

Quint had expected Jules to start shooting at him. But apparently Jules was going to be satisfied with killing Slade. Quint ran to the spot where Slade had fallen. He felt for a pulse and was amazed when he found it. Slade was still alive.

Quint got to his feet, giving no indication to Jules that he had found any spark of life in Slade. He went back to the corral where Slade and Quint had left their horses. Leading them to Slade, he carefully lifted Slade's limp body and draped it over the saddle while Jules watched in gloating triumph. Tying it there, he started toward Julesburg.

Even though Slade was alive now, it wasn't likely that he could survive the trip to town. Quint thought. But if he had asked for a wagon,

Jules would have known that Slade was still alive. Quint was sure that Jules' only objective had been to kill Slade. He might even have stolen the horses and left them in the corral where they could be easily identified just to trap Slade and kill him.

Quint fought the urge to hurry. He knew Slade needed medical attention immediately. But if he hurried, the jolting of the horses would only lessen Slade's chances of survival.

He wondered about his job now. He had been fortunate enough to hold it through the change from Jules to Slade. But now what? Maybe it was time he got out of Julesburg. But two things held him.

He still carried that half note in the heel of his boot. He wouldn't leave Julesburg until he saw what the other half of that note said. And there was Mary. He seldom missed walking down to Baxter's store after he finished work each night. Mary was always there to meet him.

He often caught himself thinking it could be like that every night only Mary would be waiting at a little home rather than at a store. He had tried to smother the thought. Any day he might be a candidate for a pine box. He had no business even thinking of Mary and a home. But the dream was there, and he knew that he could not rid himself of it easily.

This turn of events, however, would change

things. Whether or not he held his job at the station, he knew his own life was in more danger than ever. Quint was sure that Slade's reputation as a gunman had kept Judd Hurley at a distance. And it probably had the same effect on Cole Fray. Quint hadn't seen Fray lately, but he knew he wasn't far away; he wasn't a man to give up easily. The key to a fortune was in Julesburg, and he knew it; he would never leave until he got it.

Slade's reputation with a gun had been planted in Julesburg by Ficklin. The stories may have been started to frighten off anyone who had ideas of waxing fat off robbing the stages. But Slade's appearance and the way he handled himself had given substance to the stories.

But now Slade was no longer a barrier between Quint and those who would like to see him dead. Quint would have to increase his vigilance. If he didn't, he would soon be nearer death than Slade was right now.

NINE

The road back to Julesburg from the ranch where Jules had ambushed Slade seemed endless to Quint. He fought the urge to hurry. He knew that every minute Slade rode draped over that saddle was ebbing the life from him. But he was also aware that to hurry would only make the wounds bleed more and drain the life from him quicker.

So he held the horses to a walk and hoped that Slade's rugged constitution would sustain him until they reached the station. He glanced back often, but he couldn't tell whether Slade was still breathing or not. There wasn't anything he could do about it if he wasn't.

When at last he reined up in front of the station, Mike Shield came out on a trot.

"What happened?" he demanded.

"Jules," Quint said. "He stole the horses, all right, and put them in a corral at the ranch where he's been staying. When Slade went to the house to look for Jules, Jules got the drop on him and shot him."

Quint dismounted and stepped back beside Slade's horse. Mike looked at Slade, draped over the saddle, and shook his head.

"Looks like a war party of redskins got to him."

"Jules used a six-gun, then a shotgun on him,"

Quint said. He examined Slade quickly. He was still breathing, which seemed a miracle in itself.

"We'd better take him home," Quint said. "I'll need help getting him in the house."

It wasn't far from the station to the house where Slade and his wife, Virginia, lived. She saw them coming and rushed out to meet them. Quint repeated his story. He decided that Virginia Slade was a remarkable woman. She didn't go into hysterics, didn't even cry. She directed Quint and Mike as they untied the ropes that Quint had used to hold Slade on the horse and carried him inside. After they had laid him on the bed, she went after hot water while Quint sent Mike for the doctor.

Quint hurried back to the station, promising Virginia Slade that he would return soon to see how her husband was doing. With Slade near death and Mike gone for the doctor, there was no one attending the station.

When Quint checked back at the Slade home late that afternoon, he found Mary Baxter helping Mrs. Slade care for the wounded man. The doctor had done all he could and had said that Slade had an even chance of pulling through, although he couldn't explain how he could still be alive.

For two days, Slade was either unconscious or irrational. The doctor checked on him frequently, and either Virginia Slade or Mary Baxter was at his side constantly. The third day, when the fever he had contracted broke, he became rational. Those around him felt that the worst was past and that Jack Slade would live.

Late that afternoon Quint left Mike Shield in charge of the station and went over to check on Slade's progress. He had barely gotten into the house when Mary called his attention to a rider who had reined up in front of the station.

"Jules!" Quint exclaimed. "What is he doing here?"

"Maybe he came to make sure he killed Jack," Mary suggested softly.

"Possibly," Quint agreed.

He watched Jules talk to Mike Shield who had come out of the station. Jules didn't tarry long there but nudged his horse on toward Slade's house. Quint was sure now that Mary had guessed right. Jules must be half crazy, Quint decided, to ride into town like this after ambushing Slade.

Quint considered going outside and stopping Jules before he could get to the house, but Slade was awake and he had heard what they had been saying.

"Let him in," he said weakly. "I want to see him."

Quint shot a look at Slade. Slade was too weak to put up any kind of a fight. He doubted if he could even hold a gun. Quint rested a hand on his own gun as Jules dismounted and strode toward the door as if it were his own home. He came in without knocking and stared around at those inside.

After flashing looks at Quint and Mary on one side of the room and at Virginia Slade on the other, his dark eyes concentrated on Jack Slade lying on the bed.

"Hump!" he grunted after staring at Slade for a minute. "You should be dead."

Quint watched Jules for any threatening move. He didn't want to shoot a man who wasn't even shooting at him. But he would if Jules threatened Slade. Jules deserved killing. There had been great indignation around town when Quint had brought Slade in. There were men in town who would be furious when they found that Quint had not gunned Jules down.

"It will take a better man than you to kill me," Slade said, staring back at Jules.

Quint was amazed at the strength in Slade's voice. He could imagine the effort it was taking for the wounded man to generate such a show of strength.

"You ain't going to bother me none," Jules said. "I take over my station just like before. You bother me and I kill you for sure this time."

Somehow Slade managed to raise himself on one elbow. "I'll live to cut off your ears, Jules, and nail them to the wall."

For a moment, Quint thought that Jules was going to reach for his gun, but then his face broke into a big grin. “I wait for that big day,” he said sneeringly. “If you get out of that bed, you get out of this country quick.”

Jules wheeled and strode out the front door. Slade sank back on the bed, his face turning white from his effort. Both Virginia and Mary rushed to him. Quint turned to the window and watched Jules mount his horse.

Then his attention was caught by a movement over at the station. Mike Shield had been there alone when Quint left. Now he saw that there were at least two other men there. Apparently, someone had seen Jules ride in and had spread the word.

Quint switched his attention to Jules. Surely Jules would see the danger there and swing his horse around the station. But Jules obviously had no such intention. Quint guessed that Jules really believed that once he had eliminated Jack Slade, he could move back into his station and take command as before and that no one would dare challenge his right.

Quint was still watching from the window when Jules reached the station. He saw Jules arguing with the two men in front of the station. Then suddenly another man appeared in the doorway of the station, a shotgun aimed directly at Jules’ belly.

Quint ran out the door and across to the station. By the time he got there, Jules was off his horse.

The three men had surrounded him, taking his gun. Jules was swearing violently, partly in English, partly in a language Quint didn't understand.

"You think you can steal us blind, kill the man who takes your place, then come back and steal us blind again?" one man shouted. "You're going to get what's coming to you!"

Two more men came running from the main part of town. One had a rope. The other man went with one of the men standing behind Jules and found a long pole. Almost before Quint realized what they had in mind, the two men had fastened the end of the long pole to the tops of the high boxes of two freighting wagons standing beside the station. The sides of those wagons stood up higher than a man could reach.

Something inside Quint rebelled at the idea of lynching Jules. Anything that happened to him would be no more than he deserved, but hanging him with no pretense of a trial went against Quint's sense of decency.

"Let the law hang him," he suggested.

"Maybe the law would hang him and maybe it would let him go," one man retorted. "We ain't taking no chances on him getting out of this."

Quint started to move forward, but one of the men turned his gun toward him. Quint didn't doubt that he would use it. There were only five men involved, but they were as determined as a mob of a hundred men. Quint didn't press his point.

It took only a minute to get the rope around the swearing Jules' neck. Once the rope was in place, all the rage and bravado went out of the former station agent. He sputtered helplessly until his words began to make sense again. Now he was begging for his life. Thinking of the way Jules had been a few minutes ago, gloating over Slade's helplessness, Quint found the sudden change amazing.

But the begging fell on deaf ears. While one man kept an eye on Quint to make sure he didn't interfere, the others dragged Jules over under the pole across the high boxes of the freighting wagons. One man flipped the rope over the pole and pulled the end through a wheel.

Quint expected them to stand Jules on a box, then kick it out from under him. But they simply gave him a boost while the man on the rope jerked the slack through the wheel and flipped a half hitch in the rope. When the man released Jules, his feet were dangling three inches from the ground.

Quint found it hard to stand and watch Jules fight the rope and choke, but he had no choice. The man watching Quint didn't let the drama before him divert his attention.

Quint wasn't aware that any more men had arrived until he saw Blix Hurley run toward the kicking man. Curiously, nobody moved to stop Blix, and Quint realized that the actual sight of a man dying at the end of a rope had sobered the men and dampened the rage that had driven them to violence.

Blix gave the half hitch in the rope around the wheel a jerk; Jules crashed to the ground, landing in a heap. He was still gasping, but Quint wasn't sure that it wasn't just muscle reaction.

Some of the men turned and made their way back to town as if they had lost all interest in the drama. Quint stayed, but he didn't interfere with Blix working over the fallen man. Although Quint had been looking for Blix, now that he had found him, the circumstances were far from right to ask him the questions he wanted to. A couple of the men who had taken a hand in hanging Jules stayed too.

Within three minutes, Jules had begun to revive. When Blix got him on his horse, one of the men from town confronted Jules.

"You get out of town, Jules, and don't you ever show your face here again."

Jules nodded dully. "I go. I never come back."

It sounded to Quint like a solemn promise. He watched Blix lead the horse away, Jules hanging to the saddlehorn; then he went into the station where Mike Shield had stayed, keeping away from the trouble outside.

It was another day before Ben Ficklin, superintendent of the stage line, sent a man to replace Jack Slade as agent at the Julesburg station. He was a man that Quint liked on first sight. The feeling seemed to be mutual, and Quint was retained. Mike Shield also kept his job.

Slade recovered slowly. As the days went by, Quint kept an eye out for Blix and Judd Hurley. But he saw neither of them. Blix apparently had disappeared with Jules Beni. But Quint couldn't believe that he had left the country. He thought perhaps that Jules had.

Quint's desire to go on to the gold fields had faded. He wasn't a prospector. He couldn't hope to get a much better job in Denver than he had right here. And there was still that note in the hollowed-out heel of his boot. Somehow he would find a way to get the other half of the note from Gilda Ryan. He wouldn't be satisfied until he found out what Joe Linzy had hidden away, what was so important that he wouldn't trust anybody with instructions on how to find it.

But Gilda avoided him, and Quint found no opportunity to force her to bring out her half of the instructions.

As soon as Jack Slade had recovered enough that he was able to ride in a coach, he and his wife, Virginia, were put on the eastbound stage to Illinois. Slade promised he would be back. If Jules Beni was still alive when he returned, he would hunt him down and kill him. Quint didn't doubt him. Jack Slade was that kind of man.

Quint began going back to the Baxter store whenever he could find an excuse. He had seen Mary often during the time Jack Slade needed intensive care. But now that Slade was gone, Mary was back in the store.

When both Quint and his mother were invited to the Baxters' for supper one evening, Quint looked forward to a grand time. He wasn't disappointed. He was slightly irritated, however, by the questions that Lem Baxter asked. It seemed to Quint that he asked more questions than any gossip he had ever known. Yet he had never heard Lem Baxter pass along any gossip.

The questions were not personal ones, though. Personal questions wouldn't have surprised Quint, for it must be obvious now that his interest in Mary was increasing.

But Lem Baxter's questions were mostly about Quint's work at the station and the new man who had come to take Slade's place. He also asked about Jules, Quint hadn't heard any more about Jules. But there had been some stage robberies to the west along the Rocky Ridge section of the road. Those robberies had some of the marks of Jules Beni, except that they were being staged by a gang now. Jules had usually worked alone.

"I think it is Jules," Lem Baxter said, puffing on his pipe. "He knows he can't ruin the stage line alone. But with a gang, he can steal enough that even Russell, Waddell, and Majors can't stand the losses."

"Who could get along with Jules well enough to belong to a gang he was bossing?" Quint said.

Baxter grinned. "You've got a point there. But the whole gang is probably birds of a feather."

Quint moved cautiously along the street as he took his mother back to the boarding house. Ever since Judd and Blix Hurley left the wagon train, he had taken precautions each time he stepped outside after dark. Quint was sure they were still around waiting for a chance to kill him. And Julesburg's dark streets offered plenty of opportunities.

He saw his mother to her room, then went to his own. The minute he touched the door knob he realized something was wrong. The locks on the doors at the boarding house were faulty at best, but still he always turned the lock on his door when he left. The door wasn't locked now.

There was no light inside the room. Whoever had forced the lock might be gone. Or he might be waiting for Quint to step inside. He drew his gun, thinking that anyone inside would know that he was out in the hall. Quint hadn't been particularly quiet.

He kicked the door open, dodging to one side. But no gun roared as he expected. For a moment there was absolute silence, then a woman's voice came out of the darkness.

"Don't start shooting."

Quint stepped inside, conquering his surprise. "The candle's on the bureau. Light it."

A match scratched, and its flare pierced the darkness. Quint saw Gilda Ryan move to the bureau and touch the flame to the candle.

"What are you doing here?" Quint demanded. Then he saw her face. There was a big bruise on her right cheek bone, and her right eye was purple and swollen almost shut. "What did you tangle with?"

"Cole Fray and Russ Spark," Gilda said, and Quint detected the hatred in her voice.

"After your half of the note?" he guessed.

She nodded. "They got it, too."

"How did they know you had it?"

"My big mouth," Gilda said disgustedly. "I hadn't told anybody I had it. Nobody knew it but you. Then last night I had too many belts and I let it slip."

"Why didn't you come to me with that half note when I told you I had the other half? We could have found whatever Joe Linzy intended for us to have long before this."

"Sure, I know," Gilda said, holding one hand to her head. "But Cole Fray told me you had killed Joe to get his fortune and was here now to collect it. Cole didn't know about me having half the note, but he did know I was Joe's girl, and he figured I knew where he had hidden his loot."

"And you don't?"

"Do you think I'd be hanging around a town like this if I had that money? But after what Cole told me, I was afraid you'd kill me if you had to, just to get my half of that note. Cole got me drunk to get me to tell him where the money was. That's when I let it slip about the note."

"Now he'll want my half."

"You'd better believe it!"

Quint pulled off his boot. "Can you remember what your half of the note said?"

"It didn't make much sense," Gilda said. "It was ripped from top to bottom. There were even some half words."

"I know," Quint said. He took his knife from his pocket and pried on the heel of his boot. After some working, he got it off and took out the folded note. He spread it out and let Gilda look at it. He wouldn't have been surprised if she had tried to snatch it and run. But she didn't even seem to want to touch it.

"Can you remember enough of the half you had to make sense of this?" he asked.

She studied the note carefully and finally shook her head with a sigh. "I thought I had my half memorized. But I can't fit it onto this."

Quint studied her face. Was she just memorizing his half of the note so she could put the two halves together in her memory later?

"You'd better hide this pretty well," she said

after a minute. "They'll probably figure it out now that you came to Julesburg because you had the note and was looking for the other half."

Quint nodded. "I'll find a safe place for it. They wouldn't be likely to search you for the other half."

She shrank back from him. "Nothing doing. I don't want them to beat me up again." She searched his face for a minute in the flickering light. "If you get the other half of that note from Cole Fray, I figure you'll give me my share of whatever you find. You look honest. Too bad I didn't have sense enough to figure that out before."

Quint looked at the half note in his hand. "They probably won't be able to figure out any more from their half of this note than you did."

"But they will figure out that you have the other half," Gilda said. "They must know that Joe gave it to you."

"They know, all right," Quint said, remembering the letter he'd received from Fray back in eastern Kansas. "And they'll kill me to get it if they get the chance."

TEN

After Gilda left his room, Quint debated where to hide his half of Joe Linzy's instructions. The hollow heel of his boot had been a perfect place. But Gilda had seen it.

Considering his original opinion of her, he wasn't inclined to trust her implicitly. She would talk if Fray put the pressure on her again. She was deathly afraid of Cole Fray.

Quint pounded the heel back on his boot, deciding to put the note under the lining of the waistband of his pants. It wasn't an ideal place, but he couldn't think of a better one right now. He didn't want to hide it in the room. He wanted that note with him at all times.

His next move, the way he saw it, was to find Cole Fray and retrieve the half note he stole from Gilda. Once he found what Joe Linzy had hidden, he would know whether he wanted to risk remaining in Julesburg. Besides, he owed Fray and Russ Spark something for the beating they had given him when he first came to Julesburg.

But finding the pair proved to be more of a task than he had expected. He had thought they would be looking for him. But he didn't see either of them the next few days, although he spent every minute off his job searching the town and inquiring for them.

Then one night when he came to the boarding house from the station, he found Gilda waiting for him before going to work. After her beating, she hadn't avoided him as before; in fact, she made it a point to check with him frequently.

"We have a new gambler down at the saloon," she said. "Thought you might like to know. Blix Hurley."

Quint frowned. If Blix had an occupation, gambling was it. But he hadn't expected him to deal the cards professionally here. If he was working at the saloon now, that meant Quint could find him when he wanted to. And he wanted to find him right now.

Quint felt that he really had little to fear from Blix. But Judd was a different matter. Quint hadn't seen Judd since that night out at the wagon train. But he knew he was around. Blix wouldn't be here if Judd wasn't.

"Thanks for telling me, Gilda," Quint said. "I might drop down later tonight and see him."

"Don't tell him I told you he was there."

"Don't worry. A man can drop into a saloon without having to be told there is someone there he's looking for."

Quint went down the street shortly after supper. He wanted his appearance there to seem natural.

Gilda was a good source of information as to what was going on in the other half of town. He didn't want to do anything to cut off that information.

Quint didn't expect Blix to fight when he confronted him. But he did expect him to try to wiggle away without answering his questions. Blix liked to be on the winning side in any conflict, but he didn't like the dangers of actual combat.

But Quint's evaluation of the situation underwent a drastic change the moment he stepped inside the saloon. He spotted Blix almost immediately, sitting at a table with three other men playing cards. Two of those men were Cole Fray and Russ Spark.

Fray was the first one to notice Quint. He made a sign and Russ Spark looked up. Blix made a sound in his throat as if he were strangling and pushed back his chair.

"Been looking for you," Fray said, easing his chair back from the table.

"I haven't been hard to find," Quint said. "But I've been looking for you, and you've been mighty hard to find."

Fray got up. The other three at the table were quick to follow his example. Blix and the man Quint didn't know backed off hastily. Spark moved away more slowly.

"We've got a few things to talk over," Fray

said quietly, the surprise that had hit him at first fading away.

"Could be," Quint agreed.

Quint was on the alert. Fray seemed to want to talk rather than fight. That wasn't what Quint had expected. Suddenly, he understood. Spark was backing slowly away and with every step he was getting more out of Quint's vision.

"Hold it, Spark!" he snapped. "You're in this, too. Stay where I can see you."

Spark stopped and Fray frowned, a tiny crease in his forehead. But he made no move to start a battle.

"You said you were looking for me," Fray said. "What do you want?"

"A private talk with you," Quint said.

"This is as private as you're going to get it."

It was Quint's turn to frown. Fray had put him on the defensive. That wasn't the way he wanted it.

"You came to Julesburg looking for me," Quint said. "Now you've found me. I figure it's your move."

Fray shook his head. "I move only when I'm ready. I'm not ready now."

For a minute Quint had concentrated on Fray. Now he suddenly realized that had been a mistake. Spark had begun to move again, slipping farther to Quint's left.

Quint backed a couple of steps, half turning,

trying to see both Spark and Fray at once. But there was too much distance between the two.

"Get back over there with Fray," Quint said sharply to Spark.

Spark scowled and stood his ground. Fray laughed, and Quint glanced back at him.

"I don't need him to back me," Fray said.

It was then, while he was watching Fray, that Quint caught Spark's move out of the corner of his eye.

Quint's hand swept down as he wheeled toward Spark. Spark had his gun in his hand. It roared and Quint, falling back, was sure he felt the breath of the bullet snap past his head. His own gun bellowed, filling the air around Quint with acrid smoke.

Spark's gun roared again; Quint answered, aiming now as much at the sound and smoke as at Spark, for he was half hidden behind the smoke. After firing, Quint dodged back. Fray's gun was in the fracas now, but his bullet ripped into the wall behind where Quint had just been. Quint answered Fray's shot then dodged away again. Smoke was so thick around Quint now that he couldn't be sure what he was shooting at.

Quint expected another shot from Spark, but none came and he concentrated on Fray. But there were no more shots from that area either. Quint saw a man dodging along the far wall, but through the smoke, he couldn't be sure whether it was Fray or someone else, so he held his fire.

For a minute, there was no sound in the room except some shuffling feet. And soon even that stopped. The smoke drifted up to the ceiling, the air slowly clearing.

Quint saw Spark then, sprawled over a table. He looked for Fray. But he was gone. So was Blix. After making sure that neither was waiting in some corner for him to move out, he edged his way over to Spark. The man was dead, hit squarely in the chest.

Before anybody else began stirring, Quint made a quick search of Spark's pockets. He really didn't expect that Fray had trusted Spark with that half note he had stolen from Gilda, but Quint couldn't afford to pass up any possibility. Spark didn't have anything in his pockets but some coins and a couple of loose bullets for his gun. Quint knew that the note might be hidden in his clothing, but he had no chance now to check.

The only reaction to the fight that Quint met was one of complete aloofness. No one wanted to mix into it. Apparently, Russ Spark had had no close friends among the men in the saloon.

Quint remembered his original purpose, but Blix Hurley had disappeared with Cole Fray; they had been in the same game. Quint wondered if there could be some association between Fray and Blix. That would certainly complicate Quint's troubles.

Quint watched the street carefully as he returned to the boarding house. He didn't expect to see Blix again that night. But he wasn't so sure about Fray. Fray struck him as the kind who ran away only when he felt the odds would be more in his favor the next time. Fray might be waiting somewhere in ambush.

But things were still quiet when Quint reached the boarding house. There seemed to be little or no fuss over the shooting in the saloon. He wasn't surprised. There was no law here except what a man carried in his holster. Everyone kept out of the other fellow's trouble, apparently thankful it was none of his own. Quint himself had stayed in the boarding house night after night when he had heard shooting down at the saloon. The next day he might hear that a man had been wounded or even killed, but usually some fellow just in off the trail had been letting off some steam.

Quint braced a chair under the knob of his door before going to bed and kept his gun under his pillow. This was a precaution that he expected to follow from now until he and Cole Fray had a showdown.

Cole Fray was nowhere to be found the next day. Even Blix didn't show up at the saloon the next night. But the following night he was back. Quint tried to catch him, but he slipped out the moment Quint showed up.

Gilda brought Quint some news a few days

later that irritated him more than he would let anybody know. She told him she had seen Blix over at Baxter's store two evenings on her way to work.

Quint considered the situation. Of course Gilda could be lying about it. But Quint had a feeling she wasn't. Blix had always had an eye for a pretty girl. And Mary was the prettiest girl within a hundred miles, Quint was sure. But he couldn't allow himself to think that she would give a man like Blix Hurley any encouragement.

The next two evenings, he got off work as early as possible and hurried down to the store. But Blix wasn't there. Either he had never been there or had slipped away in plenty of time to avoid meeting Quint. Quint tried to tell himself that it would be a good break for him if Blix was coming around to the Baxter store. For he still wanted to corner Blix and make him tell him where Judd was. Since he couldn't catch him anywhere else, maybe he could at the store.

When Blix wasn't there the second night, Quint felt he had to inquire. Mary seemed as glad to see him as usual, but he couldn't forget what Gilda had said. Gilda had left no doubt about Blix's reason for hanging around the store.

"Has Blix Hurley been in today?" Quint asked, trying to sound casual.

"He was here not twenty minutes ago," Mary said.

"What for?" Quint asked bluntly.

"What would anybody come to a store for?" Mary countered.

"Not the same thing Blix would," Quint said darkly.

Mary spread her hands on the counter. "Dan Quint! Are you hinting that he was here just to see me?"

"I doubt if he buys many groceries," Quint said.

"What if he does come to see me?" Mary said spiritedly. "Is that any worse than you spending your time with Gilda Ryan?"

Quint frowned. "I don't spend my time with her. She brings me information now and then that is a big help to me."

"What kind of information?"

Quint considered that question. He had talked himself right into a corner. His mission here to get the other half of Joe Linzy's note was something he didn't toss around in any conversation. In fact, he hadn't mentioned it to either Mary or her father. But he had told them about Blix and Judd Hurley. He seized on this as a quick way out.

"For one thing, she told me about Blix hiring out as a gambler in the saloon."

"And about him hanging around the store, too, I suppose?"

Quint frowned again. Mary made that sound like nasty gossip. He didn't like the way this conversation was going.

"Oh, forget it," he said. "How about going out and looking at the sunset?"

She smiled. "That sounds like a much more interesting subject."

Quint couldn't notice any real difference in Mary's attitude toward him now that their argument had ended. But he couldn't rid himself of the feeling that Gilda was right. Blix Hurley was hanging around Mary. And she wasn't discouraging him.

A couple of days later, the station ran out of coffee beans. Quint volunteered to go down to Baxter's store. It was an hour before closing time, and he had the feeling that he might catch Blix there if Gilda's story was true.

He walked down the street, seeing no horse in front of the store. But as he passed the blacksmith shop, he noticed one tied behind the store. Then as he got closer to the store, he saw Blix suddenly dart out the front and around the far corner. Quint sprinted toward the horse at the back, forgetting about the coffee beans.

He reached the corner of the store just as Blix got to the horse. He knew then that he had guessed right. Blix had tied his horse behind the store so nobody, especially Quint, would see him visiting Mary.

Quint lunged at the horse and caught its bridle. Wheeling around the horse, he grabbed Blix before he could settle in the saddle. With a yank, he pulled him off the horse; Blix struck out savagely at Quint. Quint waded in, suddenly feeling like this was the ultimate goal of his life.

But the fight was a short one. Blix's fists struck only glancing blows while Quint drove one fist into Blix's stomach and the other into his face. Blix collapsed, all the fight gone from him.

"What are you doing here?" Quint demanded.

"A man can go to a store if he wants to, can't he?"

"Every day?" Quint said. "You don't buy that much grub."

Blix was beginning to recover from the blows he had taken. He seemed to realize that Quint wasn't going to pound him any more as long as he didn't show any fight. He grinned wickedly.

"There's more in that store than grub."

"You stay away from Mary!" Quint snapped.

"Let her tell me that," Blix said confidently.

"I'll have her do that," Quint said, and spun on his heel and strode around the corner of the store.

It wasn't until he was nearly to the front of the store and heard Blix's horse pound away that he remembered his original purpose. He had wanted to find out where Judd was. He had been so infuriated at Blix's insinuation that Mary was leading him on that he had forgotten all about Judd.

He stormed on around the corner of the store and onto the porch. He had let Mary soothe his feelings by denying that she had any interest whatsoever in Blix.

Mary was waiting just inside the store. “What was all the racket out back?” she asked.

“I had a little difference of opinion with Blix. He said he’d been here seeing you. Is that right?”

“What if it is? I can’t control who comes into the store and sees me.”

“You don’t have to lead him on.”

“Who says I’m leading him on?” Mary demanded. “Did you have a fight with Blix?”

“Wasn’t much of a fight,” Quint said. “I gave him a black eye.”

“Do you feel better now?” she snapped.

Quint frowned. She was angry because he had fought with Blix. Maybe Blix was right; maybe Mary was encouraging him. He just couldn’t believe she could be interested in Blix. Not a nice girl like Mary.

Maybe she was jealous of what she thought was his interest in Gilda. But he couldn’t believe that either. He hadn’t done a thing to make Mary believe he had any interest in Gilda. Anyway, she was above such a thing as leading Blix on to strike back at him.

Maybe Blix had told Mary some lies about Gilda and Quint. If Mary was interested at all in Blix, she would probably believe anything he told her. And Blix wasn’t above telling her anything to drive a wedge between Quint and her.

Quint turned and stamped out of the store. Mary wasn't silly enough to believe such lies. If she was, then he didn't want anything to do with her, anyway.

But as he strode down the street without the coffee beans, he knew that wasn't so. Nothing could make him want to stay away from Mary.

ELEVEN

A report of another stage holdup, not far from Julesburg, reached the station a couple of days later. Lem Baxter came into the station shortly after the Pony-Express rider brought the news. Quint wanted to ask him if Blix Hurley had returned to the store, but he didn't. Baxter listened to the report of the holdup, then asked Quint for his opinion.

"Think this is another one of Jules' jobs?"

Quint scratched his chin. "We haven't heard of any other gang working anywhere west of here. But he has stayed out in the Rocky Ridge area until this time, if this is Jules and his gang."

Baxter nodded. "He's a stubborn man. And not the smartest man in some ways. He seemed to think he could come right back into town and take over his old trading post after he thought he'd killed Slade. Funny how a man can think a killing will correct all the wrongs he's done."

"You think he may be working up enough courage to try to take over the station again?" Quint asked.

Baxter shrugged. "Who knows what a man like Jules will try? But it seems certain that he does have a gang of outlaws with him now. That might make him think he could take over."

"But he ought to know that the stage company would send in an army if necessary to drive him out."

"He'd never think that far ahead," Baxter said. "No more than he did when he tried to take over after shooting Slade. Most men would have left the country like a kite in a high wind. But I didn't come down here to discuss Jules Beni. I want you to hold a place for me on the stage tomorrow going east."

"Going after more supplies?" Quint asked.

Lem Baxter had made two trips east since Quint had come to Julesburg. Each time he had said he was buying supplies for his store. That puzzled Quint. It didn't seem to him that the store sold so much that Baxter needed to make special trips to order. He could send his orders by stage.

"Got to have things to sell in the store," Baxter said. "I'm getting Mrs. Mason to stay with Mary while I'm gone and help her in the store. You might look in now and then."

Quint almost said he doubted if Mary would appreciate having him drop in on any excuse. But he only nodded. He wouldn't rest easy while Lem Baxter was gone, knowing Mary and Mrs. Mason were alone. Mrs. Mason was the blacksmith's wife, a capable woman. But evidently neither Lem Baxter nor Mary had any idea of the kind of man they were dealing with when they let Blix Hurley hang around the store. Blix himself wasn't so dangerous, perhaps, but wherever Blix was, Judd Hurley would not be far away.

"I'll keep an eye on them," Quint said.

After Baxter was gone, Quint tried to find a logical reason for Baxter's trip. But he failed until he remembered that Baxter was a widower. Maybe there was a woman somewhere. Perhaps he would bring a wife back from one of these trips. At least it made more sense to Quint than buying supplies for his store. Baxter might be shy enough not to want everyone to know the real purpose for his trips east.

Lem Baxter left on the stage the next day, buying his fare only as far as Ft. Kearny. Quint knew he couldn't buy any supplies there. He'd have to go on to the Missouri River or maybe even to St. Louis to find a company that could ship what he needed. But Quint said nothing. Let Baxter handle his own affairs. If he got back in less than a week, Quint would know that he hadn't gone all the way to St. Louis.

While Baxter was gone, Quint checked frequently at the store. Mary and Mrs. Mason seemed to have everything under control. Once Quint caught a glimpse of Blix Hurley as he approached the store, but he didn't catch up with him. It was obvious to Quint, though, that Blix was hanging around Mary more than ever. She certainly must be encouraging him or even Blix would leave her alone.

Lem Baxter was back in four days. Quint said nothing about the brevity of his trip, but he knew that Baxter hadn't gone far enough to order supplies. He seemed in unusually good spirits which strengthened Quint's suspicion that a woman was the reason for Baxter's trip.

It was just two days after Baxter's return that the eastbound stage broke a wheel a short distance west of the Julesburg station. Quint realized there was trouble when he saw the driver coming into the station riding one of the lead horses. Both Quint and the station agent hurried outside.

"What happened?" Quint demanded, thinking that there must have been an Indian raid or perhaps a holdup in which the stage was wrecked and probably all the passengers killed.

"Broke a wheel," the stage driver said disgustedly. "Hit a big rock on a turn. Broke a couple of spokes; the fellow collapsed, and that was it."

"Must have been some rock," Quint said.

"It was," the driver said. "It shouldn't have happened, but it did. Got a blacksmith here to fix it?"

"Sure. Mason can do it. May take a while, though."

"Reckon it will."

"Where's your passengers? Or are you alone?"

"I'll say I'm not alone," the driver said. "Got

three passengers and a shipment of gold. First thing I thought of was that it was a holdup and that rock had been deliberately put there. But I guess it was just a freak accident."

"The guard still out there?"

"Sure. Couldn't leave that strong box unguarded."

"Better get a wagon out there and bring that in," the agent said to Quint. "If an outlaw gang is involved, they might have waited until the driver was gone to strike."

"That's possible, I reckon," the driver agreed. "But we couldn't just sit out there all night."

Quint helped Mike hitch up a team to a wagon and, with the stage driver, headed out on the road up the river. It was only about three miles to the broken-down coach. Quint half expected to find that an outlaw gang had struck while the driver was gone. But the guard was still sitting on the seat, his rifle gripped in his hands, and the three passengers were outside the coach walking around.

It took only a few minutes to load the strong box and the broken wheel onto the wagon. Then the passengers and their luggage were loaded, and Quint turned the team toward Julesburg again.

"We'll have to lay over till tomorrow, I reckon," the guard said.

"Sure," the driver said. "It will take a while to

fix this wheel. At least, there is a boarding house for the passengers."

Quint unloaded the passengers at Mrs. Ketrick's boarding house, then turned back toward the station.

"Got a safe?" the driver asked.

Quint shook his head. "I don't think there's one anywhere in town. Is there quite a bit of gold in there?"

"There sure is," the driver said. "I don't know how much, but we were told to watch it close."

"Reckon we'll have to stand guard over it tonight."

The strong box was carried inside the station and put in a corner. Quint wasn't too worried about it. If road agents had been responsible for the accident to the coach, they surely would have taken the strong box out there on the road. They wouldn't wait until the box had been moved into the station.

Nevertheless, it was agreed that a guard would be maintained throughout the night. Quint and the man who had been riding shotgun on the stage, a short, stocky man named Clint Nelson, drew the first watch until midnight. The station agent and the driver would take the second watch.

Quint was sure that half the people in town dropped in at the station before closing time. News of the stage breakdown quickly traveled over the small community. Lem Baxter lingered longest.

"Sure funny about that rock," he said after hearing the details of the accident. "If Jules was in the country, I'd figure he might have had a hand in it."

"He'd have taken the gold out there if he'd planted that rock," Quint said.

Baxter nodded. "Looks that way. But who can figure Jules? I'd sure keep a sharp eye out, anyway. Want me to help?"

Quint shook his head. "I reckon we can hold them off if anybody tries to break in. You might come running if you hear any shooting."

"I'll do that," Baxter said.

"Who was that?" Nelson asked after Baxter had left.

"Runs the store down the street," Quint said.

"He didn't look like anybody we need to watch," Nelson said. "But you can't always tell."

"Baxter's all right," Quint said. "But there could be people in town who might get itchy fingers when they think about all this gold down here not even locked in a safe."

"I reckon we've got more to watch out for from people right here in town than from some outlaw gang," Nelson agreed.

Quint thought of Blix Hurley. He would be sure to hear about this. He and Judd might try to take the gold during the night. If Cole Fray was still around, and Quint was sure he was, he might also make a try. In fact, he and Blix might team up. Quint remembered that Fray and Blix had been together the night Quint had killed Russ Spark.

As darkness closed in and the town settled down for the night, Quint grew more alert. Maybe the broken wheel had been purely accidental. But it had created a situation that invited real trouble.

"There are too many ways into this building," Nelson grumbled when he and Quint were alone.

"It isn't exactly a fort," Quint said. "Not with a door in the front and one in the back and a window on every side."

"We need four men to do a decent job of this," Nelson growled.

Quint looked at his watch frequently, holding it over close to the window where the moonlight could strike it. But time dragged slowly. In a way, he almost wished Cole Fray would make a try at the gold. Maybe, with Nelson's help, he could catch Fray. If he got his hands on Fray, he'd find that half note he stole from Gilda.

Nelson watched the back door that opened out onto the town. Quint spent most of his time at the side window, looking toward the barn and corrals. He didn't expect anyone to try to come up to the front of the building in the moonlight. There was no cover out there. On the other hand, there was good cover offered by the barn and the corrals up to within a few feet of the station. On the far side from Quint, there was a road, and across the road stood the warehouse. The road between the warehouse and the station presented a wide-open space that wouldn't be inviting to anyone trying to surprise those inside the station.

Still it was from the warehouse side of the station that the surprise came. At the first sound, Quint wheeled toward the window across the room and saw the shotgun pointed in his direction. At almost the same instant, another shotgun poked through the back window, aiming at Nelson.

"Don't move!"

Quint realized that, although he and Nelson were inside in the dark, whoever was outside had been there long enough to be accustomed to the darkness. Very likely they could see where the two guards were. At least that one shotgun was certainly pointing directly at Quint.

Even if Quint moved quickly, he couldn't escape the pellets from that scatter-gun. Quint shot a glance at Nelson. Apparently, he was thinking the same. The man at the back window was closer to Nelson than the other man was to Quint.

The man at the back window crawled in. Then the other man did the same. One man went to the front door and unlocked it. A minute later, two more men came in.

At first, Quint had thought it might be Fray

and Blix, but this was an organized effort of four men, and from the looks of things, it was going to be successful.

"Move over to that wall," one of the men snapped. "Where's the gold?"

"What gold?" Nelson asked.

"Don't try to be cute," the man snapped. "Two men don't sit up all night in a station like this guarding the merchandise."

"Shall I strike a match?" another one asked.

"No, you idiot!" the spokesman snapped back. "We don't want half the town up here. We can find the box."

Something about the voice sounded familiar, but Quint couldn't quite place it. He realized that the men were wearing masks. That was a precaution he hardly expected at night.

One of the robbers moved around the room until he found the strong box. "Give me a hand," he said. "Let's get out of here."

Two of the men took the box by the handles. One of the others moved up behind Nelson and brought his gun down across the back of his head. Nelson slumped forward without a sound.

Quint expected the same treatment, but the spokesman turned his gun directly on him. "You're coming with us. I was hoping you'd be one of the men on guard."

Suddenly, Quint recognized that voice. Judd Hurley. He hadn't heard it since that fight out at the wagon train. He had been expecting Blix. He should have known Judd would be with him. But he had no idea who the other two were. Fray might be one.

Quint knew that if he went with Judd, he would be going to his death. But with that gun pointed right at his middle, he had no choice.

"Why didn't you take the gold today when the stage broke down, Judd?" Quint asked.

For a moment there was a stony silence, apparently as Judd resigned himself to having been recognized. Then Judd swore softly.

"So you know me! Well, you're not going to blab it around. That stage breaking down was just a stroke of luck. Blix saw the passengers and the strong box brought in. The rest of us happened to be close. So we share the gold, and I get you all to myself. Real luck, if you ask me."

One man opened the front door, and the two carrying the strong box went out. Judd nodded toward the door and pushed Quint toward it. Quint knew that death was waiting for him somewhere beyond that door.

TWELVE

Outside the station, Judd called a halt while one man brought five horses from behind the warehouse across the road. Quint realized that the robbers had been smart enough to come in from the one direction that was the least likely to be guarded.

"We planned to use one horse for a pack horse," Judd said. "We'll let you ride him instead. Two of you men can carry the box between you."

While Judd checked Quint for any hidden guns, then tied his hands behind his back, another man went through Quint's pockets; he even took off his boots and looked inside. That was Cole Fray, Quint was sure, although the mask hid his face. Quint got some satisfaction from Fray's not finding the half note under the lining of the waistband of his pants.

The caravan started west, swinging out around the buildings of town, then cutting back toward the river. The two riders in the lead rode close together and held the box between them. Every few minutes they stopped and pushed the box over on the back of one of the horses while they rested their arms.

"As soon as we get far enough from town that they won't hear a shot, blast off that lock," Judd said. "Then you can put the gold in the saddle-bags and make better time."

"How about you carrying one end of this for a while?" one of the men grumbled.

"I've got other things to do," Judd said. "I'll meet you where we agreed to meet in case we had to separate."

Judd turned his horse toward the river, leading Quint's horse. None of the others complained. They had the strong box. They would probably be happy if Judd never appeared again.

Quint's mind was racing. He knew his time was running out. Judd could have only one purpose in getting Quint away from the others. He didn't want them to see him kill Quint.

Quint tested the rope holding his wrists. But there wasn't any give to the knots. Quint was sure that when Judd thought he was out of earshot of the town, he would shoot him.

"You figure on dumping me in the river?" Quint asked, probing for a hint of Judd's plans in the hope that he might turn the tables some way.

"Good guess," Judd chuckled. "Who can prove that you didn't get drunk and fall in the river? A drowned man tells no tales."

"One with a bullet hole in him does," Quint said.

"A drowned man doesn't have a bullet hole in him," Judd said.

Quint knew then how he was to die. When his body was found, nobody could prove that he hadn't drowned accidentally.

For a quarter of a mile, Judd led Quint's horse along the bank of the river. Then they came to a place where, even in the moonlight, Quint could see that the water close to the bank was dark and deep. The South Platte was normally a shallow stream, rippling over sand bars. But here it was deep and swirling; here a man could drown.

Quint realized that Judd had known right where he was going. Perhaps he had his camp out here somewhere. He hadn't shown up in town or, at least, Quint hadn't seen him there. Yet he had been close enough when Blix wanted to find him.

Judd drew rein and turned his gun on Quint. "Get down. This is as far as we go."

"I'm satisfied right here," Quint said. "When they find me, I want them to find a bullet hole in me."

"It's not going to be that way," Judd said, the gloating in his voice replaced by determination.

For a moment, Judd stared at Quint, but Quint didn't stir. Then, with an angry oath, Judd swung out of the saddle. Quint knew that Judd could jerk him out of the saddle easily enough. Judd was a big man, and Quint had his hands tied behind his back.

But the instant that Judd started to swing off his horse, Quint jammed his heels into his horse's flanks. Judd, half out of the saddle, couldn't use his gun.

Quint's horse, surprised by the sudden kick, leaped forward. The suddenness of the move allowed him no chance to change his direction and he crashed into Judd's horse.

Judd was flung sideways directly into the path of Quint's horse. Quint drove his heels into his horse's sides again. The horse snorted and lunged forward once more. Judd spun around, trying to avoid the horse. He was almost even with Quint's right stirrup when the horse ended his plunge. The horse, reins dragging, stopped still, every muscle quivering.

Quint jerked his foot out of the stirrup and kicked at Judd with all his strength. His toe caught Judd in the shoulder and rocked him backward. Judd yelled and tried to catch his balance. But he had no chance. His gun went flying and splashed into the river. An instant later, Judd followed it.

Quint swung his body around; the horse, settling down after the two hard kicks in the sides, obeyed the signal and turned. Quint kicked him into a trot, the fastest gait he could get out of him with the reins dragging. The horse moved along, his head turned far to one side so he wouldn't step on the reins.

At the edge of town, Quint spoke sharply to the horse, making him stop. Then he dismounted, a difficult job with his hands tied behind his back.

Once on the ground, Quint ran to the station where a light was now shining. Either Nelson had regained consciousness or the station agent and stage driver had come to take their turn at guard. Quint was met at the door by the driver, a gun in his hand. In a minute, Quint was untied and had told his story. The gold was gone, and it would be daylight before any attempt could be made at tracking the robbers.

Quint stayed at the station the next day while a posse of men tried to trail the robbers, but the tracks had disappeared as completely as a morning fog. The posse was back by noon, discouraged and disgusted. It was just another of the gold shipments that had to be marked up as lost.

Quint knew that the stage company was not going to write off those lost shipments. But their move surprised Quint.

One morning, Jack Slade and his wife stepped off a westbound stage. Quint hadn't supposed that Slade was well enough recovered from his wounds to be able to travel. But he looked as fit as he had the first time he had gotten off the stage here at the station.

"Are you going to take over the station here again?" Quint asked after welcoming Slade.

Slade shook his head. "I've been appointed superintendent of the Rocky Ridge section of the line. That's where Jules has been holding up the stages. My main reason for coming back here is to get Jules."

"You expect to get him yourself?"

"I figure on it," Slade said positively.

"He seems to have a gang with him now," Quint said. "That may be more than one man can handle."

"If I find he's got too big a gang, I'll get a gang of my own. I'm going to get him."

Quint didn't doubt that Slade would do just what he said he would. Quint had never heard more determination in anyone.

Slade and his wife stayed over a day before going on west. Slade had left some loose ends here that he wanted to tie up.

In the afternoon the westbound stage pulled into the station for a change of horses. Quint was helping Mike with the horses when the comparative silence of the afternoon was split by the thunder of hoof-beats.

"What's going on?" Mike yelled, stopping the fresh horses at the corral gate on his way to the coach.

"Indians!" somebody from the station shouted.

Quint saw them then. There were a dozen, at least, and they were charging down on the station from the hills to the south. They evidently had moved silently until they were discovered. Now they were yelling and waving their rifles as they drove their ponies forward.

Most of the passengers on the coach had already entered the station while the teams were being changed. But one man was just getting out of the coach now. Quint ran to him and helped him inside. Bullets were snapping around as the raiders began using their rifles. But their accuracy from the backs of running horses was strictly a matter of luck.

Mike led the horses back into the corral, closed the gate, then ran into the barn. Quint was inside the station now with the frightened passengers, the stage driver, the shotgun guard, and the station agent.

"We can whip them," the guard shouted. "There's only a dozen. There's almost that many of us."

From behind the counter, Quint grabbed a rifle which was kept loaded, ready for any emergency. There had been constant reports of Indian unrest up and down the trail, but no real outbreak. This was the first assault that he had heard of on any travelers or station for a long time.

"Can't figure why they'd tackle a station like this," the driver said.

"Probably figured to catch us by surprise where we couldn't fight back," the guard said. "On the trail we'd have been watching for them. But not here. Good thing I brought my rifle in with me."

"I didn't," the driver said.

Quint made a quick survey. Only three men had

rifles—the guard, the station agent, and himself. Except for a couple of hand guns, the rest were unarmed. Maybe the Indians hadn't been so foolish in their planning.

Quint concentrated on the raiders. Some were riding back and forth well out of six-gun range and beyond the accuracy of the rifles which they were firing with little effect. However, Quint caught glimpses of three or four who seemed to be sneaking in closer, using the coach as a shield.

Quint concentrated his fire on those figures, but he couldn't get a clear shot because of the coach. When he stood up, a bullet slapped into the window frame a few inches from his head and made him duck back down.

"Never saw anything like that," the guard said. "Those redskins away out there ain't going to get close enough for us to hit them. And what are those others after? Are they planning to burn the coach?"

"We'll make it hot for them when they get close enough to expose themselves," Quint said.

But the raiders got close to the coach without exposing themselves, and two of them made a dash for it. It was then that Quint realized what they were after, the strong box. The two raiders still lying out in the grass kept up a steady fire, making it dangerous for anyone inside to show himself long enough to shoot at the two climbing up on the coach. They were using revolvers now and evidently had several guns, so they wouldn't have to reload.

Once the two men got down with the box, they began dragging it hurriedly away. The other two kept up their steady fire, aiming at the window and door so that no one dared take time for more than a snap shot at the raiders.

"Those aren't Indians," Quint said positively as the bandits retreated beyond effective range.

"I was thinking that," the guard said. "No Indian gives two whoops in a barrel about gold. They'd have wanted rifles and maybe scalps. All those fellows wanted was the gold."

"Those are Indians out there riding back and forth," the driver said. "But they didn't seem to have any real heart for the raid."

"This wasn't their kind of raid," Quint said. "The outlaws probably hired them with a promise of whiskey."

Slade came running in the back door of the station. He had been down in the saloon when the shooting started. The battle had lasted only a few minutes, Quint realized now that it was over.

Slade took one look at the raiders, all mounted now and moving away. "Jules!" he spit out.

"Think so?" the driver asked.

"I sure do," Slade said. "I think all our trouble along this line from here through the Rocky Ridge section is Jules' work. The idea of robbing the stage right here at Julesburg sounds like Jules. He'd think this was real cute."

Quint saw the logic. Jules would delight in raiding this station and stealing the gold right out from under their noses. It would show his superiority and contempt for those who had deposed him.

"Let's get after them," Slade shouted.

Quint ran out to the corral and got his horse. Others followed, and soon a half-dozen men from town joined them. The raiders were gone, disappearing into the hills to the southwest.

Slade and Quint led the makeshift posse into the hills. The trail was plain and easy to follow as it turned straight west once it was safely south of town. A few miles southwest of the station, the raiders had crossed the river.

"Heading back to the foothills," Slade predicted.

Quint realized that the raiders were headed in the direction of the Rocky Ridge section of the stage line where so many holdups had been reported lately. Slade had probably guessed right. Quint wondered if Judd and Blix Hurley had been two of the raiders. He had concluded that it had been Jules' gang, or at least part of it, that had raided the station the night when Judd had almost killed him.

Darkness overtook them just a short distance west of the river. The raiders had broken up into three small groups west of the river, and the posse was confused on which trail to follow.

"Better give it up," Slade concluded at last. "I'll get Jules myself before long. I'll find the gold he's been stealing, too. But we won't catch anybody tonight, not with them splitting up like this."

Quint was glad to turn back. He had an idea he wanted to check out. Like Slade, he knew they weren't going to catch anybody now. But he was going to find out if Blix was at his gambling table tonight.

It was getting late when Quint got back to Julesburg, but he rode straight to the saloon. Dismounting, he hurried inside. Disappointment hit him when he saw Blix at his gambling table. As usual, the minute Blix saw Quint, he got up hurriedly and went through a rear door.

Quint started after him. Apparently he hadn't been on the raid this afternoon. But he could tell Quint where Judd had been. Before he got to the door where Blix had disappeared, however, Gilda cut him off.

"The boss doesn't want you running Blix out of here," Gilda said softly to Quint. "Blix is bringing in quite a lot of business, but he runs every time he sees you."

"He's got a reason to," Quint said. "But I've got some questions to ask him, boss or no boss."

Gilda held his arm. "Ask me. Maybe I can answer."

"I doubt it," Quint said. "I wanted to ask Blix where Judd Hurley was today."

Gilda shrugged. "I can't answer that. But Blix himself was gone all afternoon, the boss said."

"Gone?" Quint turned to face Gilda. "When did he get back?"

"Not more than half an hour ago. He didn't give any excuse, just took his chair and got a game going."

Quint nodded. "That's all I need to know. I reckon Blix was with Judd today."

"You'd better be careful," Gilda warned. "I heard Blix tell the boss one day that he was going to kill you if you kept bothering him."

"He may try," Quint said. "But two can play at that game."

THIRTEEN

Jack Slade and his wife came to the station the next day ready to leave on the westbound stage for Latham at the southeast end of the Rocky Ridge section of the line. Slade promised Quint that he would let him know as soon as he found out whether Judd Hurley was in Jules' gang.

"I'm sure Judd was in that raid yesterday," Quint said. "But I'm not sure that it was Jules' outfit."

"I think it was," Slade said, "even though Jules raids mostly along the Rocky Ridge section. Of course it's possible that Judd Hurley has his own gang."

Quint nodded. "Judd was in the gang that stole that gold shipment from the station here not long ago. I don't know whether Jules was in that or not. I do know that there weren't any holdups on the Rocky Ridge stretch during the days just before and after that raid. It could have been Jules."

"When I locate that gang's hideout, I may have to have help to take it, more than I can get there. If so, I'll come back."

"Count me in on that," Quint said quickly. "Especially if Judd and Blix Hurley are in the gang."

The stage from the east showed up then and Quint went to help Mike get the fresh horses ready. The horses weren't all harnessed as they usually were when the stage came in. Quint frowned as he saw Mike fumbling with the hame straps at the bottom of the collar on one of the horses.

"What's wrong, Mike?" he asked.

"Nothing," Mike said.

But Quint knew that there was something wrong. Mike's voice was tight and high-pitched, and it took three efforts for him to get the hame strap buckled.

Quint moved around where he could see Mike's face. "Something's bothering you, Mike. What is it?"

"Nothing, I told you," Mike said sharply.

Quint frowned. It was plain enough that Mike didn't want to talk about it. Quint had no business prying. But he felt that he knew Mike well enough now, after working with him so long, that he had a right to know. Maybe he could help.

"You can't fool me, Mike," Quint said. "Something has got you so worked up you'd mix gunpowder with pepper and not know the difference."

"Maybe you'd be worked up, too, if you knew you were going to be killed."

Quint frowned. "Who's going to kill you?"

"I ain't saying," Mike said. "The more I say, the quicker I'll be killed."

"How can anybody help you if you won't say who's threatening you?"

"I don't figure anybody can help me," Mike said. "Now get busy with these horses. That stage is ready to pull out."

Quint said no more. But he was thinking furiously. Who could have threatened to kill Mike Shield? And why? Obviously the threat carried real weight with Mike. Quint had never seen a man more frightened.

Quint couldn't think of a single reason why anyone would want to kill Mike Shield. He considered him a man no one would ever want to harm.

The horses were hitched to the coach, and the stage rolled on to the west, carrying Jack and Virginia Slade toward their new home. When the stage was gone, Quint again tried to talk to Mike; Mike cut him off abruptly, leaving no room for reopening the subject.

Quint went down to the saloon as soon as he was off work, but Blix was not at his gambling table. Perhaps he had seen Quint coming sooner than usual and made his exit before Quint reached the door. When Quint saw Gilda, who had apparently come down to work earlier than usual, he went over to the table where she was sitting.

"Where's Blix today?"

"I don't know," Gilda said. "I came down early

today, figuring on asking him a few questions myself. But Joe says he hasn't been in all day. In fact, he hasn't seen Blix since he left last night when you showed up."

Quint rubbed his chin. "Maybe he's made enough money and doesn't need to work for a living."

"Joe blames you for Blix's leaving," Gilda said. "He figures if you'd have left him alone, Blix would have stayed on the job. It's going to hurt Joe's business."

"I feel for him," Quint said sarcastically. "If Blix comes back, will you let me know?"

"Sure thing, Dan," Gilda said.

Quint went outside and angled across the street to Baxter's store. If Blix hadn't shown up there, it was a cinch that he had left town.

If he was gone, Quint was sure he knew where. He'd try to catch up with the gang that had staged that raid on the station yesterday. Quint guessed that Blix had come back to the saloon merely to establish an alibi in case he was connected with the robbery. That his absence during the afternoon had been noticed, however, blew his alibi to bits.

Quint entered the store. Mary and Lem Baxter had no customers, so Quint wasted no words getting to the purpose of his visit.

"Has Blix Hurley been in?"

A tiny frown tugged at Mary's brow. "I suppose you'd like to fight with him if he was here?"

"Not a bad idea," Quint said. "But that wasn't what I had in mind."

"Well, he hasn't been in here all day," Mary said. "You'll have to look somewhere else for him."

"Know where I might find him?" Quint asked.

Mary shook her head. "No. Can't your friend across the street help you?"

Quint frowned. That Mary tried to place the blame for the cooling of their friendship on his supposed interest in Gilda irritated him almost as much as her obvious interest in Blix.

"She knows better than to spend her time with the likes of Blix Hurley," Quint said.

He turned and hurried out of the store. He didn't want to argue with Mary. He had done it too often lately; it always left a bad taste in his mouth. She may have decided in favor of Blix's companionship over his, but he still didn't want to say anything that would build a permanent barrier between them.

Every day for the next two weeks, Quint checked at the saloon for the return of Blix Hurley, but he had simply disappeared. When Quint occasionally stopped in at the store, he didn't bring up the subject of Blix. But each time he listened and watched closely. He was convinced that Blix had not been there.

Then Slade came in on the eastbound stage. Quint sensed the excitement when Slade got out of the coach. Quint hurried through the chore of helping Mike with the horses. Mike had said no more about the threat to kill him and had gradually returned to near-normal behavior. As soon as he could leave the work to Mike, Quint went inside the station where Slade had gone.

"I found Jules," Slade said when he saw Quint.

"Did you bring him in?"

Slade shook his head. "I'm no coward, but I'm no fool, either. Jules has a gang with him. I don't know just how many men. I do know there are at least four. I found the spot where he hangs out not far from one of our stations."

"Need some help going after him?"

Slade grinned. "You asked for the job of helping me, remember? Well, I'm taking you up on that."

"When are you leaving?"

"As soon as I can get some men to go with me. I thought about getting some men out there, but I wanted men who really had a bone to pick with Jules. I figure it's not going to be easy taking him."

"You can find plenty of men like that here at Julesburg," Quint said. "Where is the hideout?"

"Up in the edge of the hills," Slade said. "I figure we'll take the next stage back west. We'll get horses at the station closest to their hideout, then go after the gang from there. Bring your own gun and ammunition."

Quint quickly made arrangements with the station agent to take off work for a few days, then headed for the boarding house to tell his mother and get what he would need for the trip. Before he headed back to the station, he went down to the store.

He was sure that Blix and Judd Hurley would be with Jules. That made the prospect of rounding up the gang more enticing. But he had to be certain that Blix hadn't returned to Julesburg. If he had, Mary and Lem Baxter would know.

Mary wasn't in sight when Quint went in. Lem Baxter was behind the counter, but he came out as soon as he saw Quint.

"Slade's back," Quint announced.

"Thought something like that was up," Baxter said, "from the look on your face. Did he find Jules?"

Quint nodded. "Found him with a gang. I'm going back with him to help round up the gang."

"Who did he say was in the gang?"

"He didn't know," Quint said. "Only that there were at least four."

"When's he heading back?"

"Soon as the westbound stage comes in. You haven't seen Blix today, have you?"

Baxter shook his head. "Not likely to, either."

Quint hesitated. Finally he said, “Tell Mary I’ll see her when I get back.”

“Sure, I’ll tell her,” Baxter said absently.

Quint went back to the station. Slade had found another volunteer named Benson. Quint barely knew him, but he did know that he was a handy man with a gun. He’d be a help on a mission like this.

A half hour before the westbound stage was due, Slade was back at the station, impatient to start.

“We’ll need more men than this, won’t we?” Quint asked.

“We can get one or two there if we need them,” Slade said. “But with two like you who really want to get Jules, the three of us can handle the whole gang if we have to.”

Quint wasn’t so sure about that, but he certainly wasn’t about to back out. Before the stage arrived, Lem Baxter came hurrying into the station, carrying a small bag and wearing a gunbelt. In his other hand, he had a rifle.

“You look like you’re heading off for a war,” Quint said in surprise.

“I am in a way,” Baxter said. “I figured on hooking on with you and Slade if you’ll let me.”

“The more the merrier,” Slade said, looking at Baxter with a puzzled grin. “But what’s this sudden urge to bring Jules to heel?”

“I’ve got plenty of reason,” Baxter said. “I

reckon I might as well tell you. If we corral Jules, my job will be over, anyway."

"Your job?" Quint exclaimed.

"That's right. I'm working for the Leavenworth and Pike's Peak Express Company the same as you and Slade are. Only nobody knows about it. My store down the street is just a front to keep anybody from suspecting there was a Company spy in town."

"Do you mean you were spying on Jules?" Slade asked.

"How do you figure the company got all that information about Jules?" Baxter asked. "They even knew some of the things that Jules had stolen. I gave Ben Ficklin that information. They had no proof at all that Jules was robbing the stages until I gave it to them. That's when they brought you in, Slade."

Slade nodded. "I did sort of wonder how Ficklin knew so much about Jules and what he had stolen from the company."

"I kept watch on Jules and reported everything he did. Now that you're about to bring Jules to bay, I figure I've got a right to be in on the kill."

"Reckon you have," Slade agreed.

"Were you going back to make reports to Ficklin when you made those trips east?" Quint asked, suddenly beginning to fill in some of the pieces that hadn't made sense before.

"Sure," Baxter said. "That story about going out to order supplies for the store was just a blind. I was only going out where I could send messages without anybody here seeing them."

"Where did you go?" Quint asked.

"Ft. Kearny usually."

"Say," Quint said, a new idea hitting him. "Do you know who is in Jules' gang now?"

"I know some of them, at least," Baxter said. "Your stepfather, Judd Hurley, is one."

"And Blix, too?" Quint asked.

"That's right. Also a man named Fray."

Quint nodded. "That's what I wanted to know. I'd go after that gang now if I had to go alone. Did you find all this out from Blix?"

"Mary did," Baxter said. "She has been working with me. When you first started working for Jules, we tried to be real friendly with you so you'd tell us what Jules was doing."

Quint nodded, feeling a little sick inside. "I guess I was a pretty good gossip, wasn't I?"

"You kept us posted," Baxter said. "But I'm afraid Mary found other interests in you than just information about Jules."

"She probably found the same interests in Blix," Quint said.

Baxter shook his head. "She hates him, but she had to be overly nice to him to get him to talk. He told us about Jules' plans and that he and Judd and Fray were running with Jules. We don't know whether there are more in the gang or not."

"Why didn't she tell me what she was doing?" Quint demanded.

"Because I told her not to. The less you say when you're prying information out of someone, the less apt he is to get wind of what you're doing."

"I suppose so," Quint said with a sigh. But he felt better than he had for some time. He wanted to talk to Mary right away. He owed her an apology for thinking she was infatuated with Blix Hurley. "I want to run up and see Mary before we start," he said.

Slade vetoed that. "The stage is coming. If you want to go with us after Jules, you'll have to come now."

"Anyway, Mary is over at Mrs. Thompson's now," Baxter said. "Mrs. Thompson is sick. I had to lock the store. I left a note for Mary. She'll understand why I have to go on this mission."

Quint looked out the front window. The stage was rolling in from the east. He fought the urge to find Mary so he could apologize and get back in her good graces. He just couldn't afford to miss the chance to go after Jules, the Hurleys, and Cole Fray. He had to find Fray and get that half note he had stolen from Gilda.

He hurried outside to help Mike. He found him as nervous and butterfingered as he had been the day Slade had left for the Rocky Ridge section two weeks ago. All his fears seemed to have returned.

Quint wondered about that, but he had no time to ponder over it. It was time now to go after Jules and his gang. Quint hoped he would find some answers to the puzzles that had plagued him ever since Joe Linzy had been killed.

FOURTEEN

When the horses were hitched to the stage, Mike turned to Quint before he climbed into the coach and gripped his hand.

"Get Jules and his whole gang," he said.

Quint detected more than just well-wishing in Mike's words. He looked at the stableman closely. Mike was almost trembling.

"We'll get them," Quint promised. "Maybe you ought to come along."

Mike shook his head. "My job is here. Anyway, I probably couldn't stand the riding you'll have to do once you get on the gang's trail."

Quint nodded. Mike was probably right about that. He had never been in the Rocky Ridge section, but he knew it ran through the edge of the mountains. That meant it would probably be pretty rough riding. And if they didn't surprise the gang, it might very well end in a chase. That could be a rough ride.

Quint climbed into the stage. There was only one passenger coming from the east. It was a good thing, Quint thought. The four men boarding at Julesburg just about filled the coach.

As Julesburg dropped out of sight behind the coach, Quint kept thinking that he should have taken time to see Mary. He had misjudged her, and it weighed on his mind. She had a right to be angry with him. But he had had no chance to apologize. Now he might never get the chance. This wasn't exactly a picnic he was going on with Slade and Lem Baxter.

"How long do you figure it will take to round up Jules' gang?" Quint asked.

"Not long if we're lucky," Slade said. "I know where their headquarters are. Of course they may not be there, and we may have to wait for them. Or we may have to run them down. The only thing I'm sure of is that we're going to get them."

Quint knew that it was Jules that Slade was after. He doubted if Slade would be so eager to corner the rest of the gang. It was the rest of the gang that mattered more to Quint. If Judd and Blix Hurley could be captured and put behind bars for a long term, he could actually relax for the first time in months.

And then there was Cole Fray. Fray should have the other half of the note that Quint still had tucked inside the lining of the waistband of his pants. Quint would find that half note if he caught Cole Fray. And, according to Lem Baxter, if they got all of Jules' gang, they'd get Fray, too.

Slade's motive was revenge, and Jules was his target. But with Quint, it was more like survival. There were three men in Jules' gang who wanted him dead. This could turn out to be the showdown that Quint had known was inevitable.

Quint was fascinated by the little station where they got off the stage. It was built of logs—a long, low structure well up on the side of a ridge overlooking a beautiful valley. Quint found himself wishing he could live in a place like this. But he hadn't come here to live; he had come to track down a gang of outlaws. Slade didn't let anybody forget the purpose of their mission.

Personal determination drove the men Slade had recruited in Julesburg. Even the fourth man in the party, Benson, had a personal score to settle with Jules. His brother had been a guard on one of the stages held up out at Devil's Dive. He had been killed and Benson was sure that Jules was the murderer.

"We'll take the trail in time to get there at dawn tomorrow," Slade announced when they had taken their things off the stage.

"Won't Jules get wise and pull out?" Baxter asked.

"I don't think so," Slade said. "He doesn't know I located his headquarters. I never got close to it, just close enough to be sure what it was and to know at least four men were staying there."

"What time will we leave?"

"About midnight," Slade said. "We'll hit the hay early."

Quint found that he was too nervous to sleep when he went to bed on the floor at one end of the station. When morning came, according to

Slade's calculations, they'd be surrounding Jules' headquarters. Quint had the uneasy feeling that everything wasn't going to go exactly as planned.

He finally did get to sleep and was roused by Slade, walking among them, nudging them with his toe.

"Time to hit the saddle," he said. "The cook has some hot grub for us. We'll saddle up before we eat."

Quint went out with the others and saddled the horse Slade indicated. It was a good horse. There was practically no light, but Quint could see that all four of the horses being saddled were long-boned rangy animals—meant for a long chase, if necessary, Quint decided. Probably Slade wasn't as confident of a complete surprise as he tried to sound.

The breakfast was good, but Quint barely tasted it. Slade had some lunches packed for each man to take. Then they were outside mounting up. Quint wore a heavy jacket against the sharp cold in the night air. But part of the chill he felt came from the cold lump in the pit of his stomach. This was the day he had been waiting for. If this raid was successful, Quint's mission to Julesburg could be completed before the day was over.

Slade led the way out into the dark. Quint didn't question where Slade was going. He had probably planned this in his mind over and over. Quint had expected at least a dozen men to go with Slade. But there were just the four of them: Slade, Baxter, Benson, and Quint. They would have to depend on surprise. Slade apparently relied on the personal determination of each man to balance the scales.

The hideout of the gang wasn't too far from the station, Quint decided when Slade reined up and cautioned them to be quiet. They hadn't come many miles, Quint was sure.

"Their hideout is over in the next valley," Slade said softly. "I don't know whether they post a night guard or not. We've got to expect that they do. We'll go around to the south and come through a low pass there. There is a better pass right ahead of us, but if they do have a guard, that's where he'll be. Ride slow and be as quiet as you can."

Slade reined his horse to the south and the others followed. They moved slowly now. They had plenty of time before daylight, Quint was sure, although he didn't know what time it was. There was only the low thump of the horses' hoofs on the ground and the creak of saddle leather in the night. When a horse occasionally hit a rock with his hoof, the sound was shockingly loud in the quiet night.

They moved in a semicircle. Quint was aware of the change in direction as he now and then glanced up at the stars. Finally Slade drew rein again. Quint realized that they were facing a valley, although he couldn't see any of the details.

"Their hideout is across the valley under an overhanging cliff," Slade said. "It's hard to see even in daylight if you don't know where to look. We'll fan out. They can't get out the back way because of the cliff. We'll spread out among the willows along the creek in front of them. Let's go."

It sounded like a simple, foolproof plan. But what if there were a couple of guards out? When they heard the commotion down at headquarters, they would come in from the rear. Slade's men would be trapped.

But Slade had considered that possibility, too. Once in the valley, he revealed his plan. He would take one man at a time and station him where he wanted him to be when the dawn light filtered down into the valley.

"I'll check that other pass to see if they have a guard out," Slade said. "Then I'll take up my position. Don't make a move until I give the signal."

"What kind of a signal?" Baxter asked.

"I'll fire the first shot. When I do, everybody open up. Make them think there are a dozen men out here."

"Are you going to demand a surrender?" Benson asked.

"I don't think they know what the word means,"

Slade said. "They'll come out fighting. It will be them or us."

Quint guessed that Slade was hoping it would be that way. Quint doubted very much if they would all come out fighting as Slade thought. If Blix Hurley was there, he'd be much more likely to come out begging, with his hands in the air.

Just before Slade took Benson to his post, Quint asked, "How many do you expect?"

"Four, maybe six, maybe a dozen," Slade said. "It makes no difference. We'll clean them out if there are a hundred."

Slade moved off into the dark with Benson. He was back in five minutes and led Quint forward. Quint was stationed in a thick clump of willows just across the creek from the spot where they had stopped. Slade told him that the cabin and corrals were almost directly in front of him.

Quint settled down to wait after Slade left. He tried to guess how long it would take to get Lem Baxter placed and for Slade to check if Jules had a guard at the pass. Quint knew that Slade had planned carefully. He wouldn't let dawn catch him unprepared.

It took longer for dawn to reach into the valley than Quint expected. The tops of the mountains began to catch the light long before the pitch darkness in the valley started to melt away. The tops of the mountains were beginning to glow with the early rays of the sun when Quint saw the first stir at the cabin. He guessed that Jules hadn't had a guard out, or if he had, Slade had found him and silenced him before he could sound any alarm.

The long cabin ahead of Quint was low and shoved back under an overhanging cliff. To the cabin's left was a long corral with several horses in it. The corral was also mostly under the cliff. It was a well camouflaged hiding place; Quint wondered how Slade had ever located it. Possibly by tracking the raiders after they had hit a stage somewhere along the line close to the station, he guessed.

The first man out of the cabin was a man Quint didn't know. He felt disappointed. Maybe this wasn't Jules' gang. Or maybe Jules didn't have the Hurleys and Cole Fray with him now. Or perhaps he had a lot of men, more than Slade's men could handle.

Then Quint saw a man come down from above the house, and he realized that the guard Slade had feared had been up there. On the cliff, the guard could easily see any movement in the valley below or in either pass. Quint was thankful for the dark night. If it had been light enough for the guard to detect their movements, he would have alerted the men in the cabin below.

Suddenly, the quiet of the early morning was shattered by a shot. The man who had just come out of the cabin spun around and flopped to the ground. Quint was sure from the way he fell that he was dead.

That shot would have come from Jack Slade. Quint realized that there was going to be no opportunity given for surrender. Slade was here to kill everyone in that cabin.

The guard who had just come down from the cliff above the cabin made a long rolling dive toward the cabin wall. The door jerked open, and the man scrambled inside. With his revolver, Slade fired three times at the man as he tried to get inside. Other guns opened up now; Quint started shooting, too. He had been shocked by the deadliness of that first bullet. He had expected Slade's first shot to be a signal to the rest of his men to begin shooting, nothing else.

Suddenly, shots from the window and the half-open door of the cabin sent a thunder of sound echoing across the valley. Quint realized that there were several men inside the cabin. It must have taken eight or ten guns to fire that many shots so fast.

Quint realized that what had been planned as an ambush could very well turn into a fight for survival for the attackers. The only way the four men could get away from the cabin without exposing themselves to certain death would be to slip away up or down the little stream among the willows.

But there was even less chance for the men in

the cabin to escape. There was very little cover right in front of the cabin.

Then a rifle began roaring out at the far end of the corral, and Quint realized that there must be a door along the side of the cabin that they couldn't see from along the creek. Somebody had slipped out of the cabin and was crawling along behind the corral. If the outlaws could get out there, maybe they could also get out over the cliff or into a crevice leading down to the creek.

Slade apparently figured the same way, for Quint was aware now that his gun was barking from farther down the creek. Slade was moving out to meet just such a move.

Quint had to keep low because the men in the cabin had located his hiding place and were splintering the willows around him with bullets. But he was down in a little depression; as long as he stayed there, the shots from the cabin would snap harmlessly through the trees above him.

Then, as unexpected as Slade's first shot must have been to the outlaws, six or seven men poured through the door of the cabin like water out of an overturned jar. One man fell as a bullet cut him down. But the shots from the willows were scattered and too hastily aimed. The rest of the men reached the corral.

A minute later, the corral gate swung open and men, hugging the bare backs of horses, poured out. Two were knocked off their horses as they charged along the base of the cliff. But the others got away.

Quint had been so surprised that he hadn't been able to recognize any of the men making the break. He wondered if Judd and Blix Hurley and Cole Fray were among them. Maybe one of them had been knocked off his horse.

Quint wheeled back toward the spot where they had tied their horses. He expected to see the horsemen come roaring back at them any instant, but to all appearances, they had kept riding.

"Suppose they ran out?" Baxter asked as he reached the horses, panting from his run.

"Might be they didn't have any idea how many of us there were and they panicked," Benson said. "Where's Slade?"

Quint turned back toward the willows. He saw Slade then, crawling up the slope from the willows toward the corral. He was moving toward a man who had been knocked off his horse.

"We'd better see what he's doing," Quint said and started in a crouching run toward Slade.

Quint wasn't sure how seriously wounded the two men were who had been knocked off their horses. And at any minute, he expected the men who had escaped to return to take up the battle again.

But there were no shots fired as he ran through the willows toward Slade. Before he got out of the willows, he saw Slade get to his feet and run up the slope toward the man who was rolling around, obviously in great pain.

Quint reached the scene shortly after Slade arrived. Quint saw then that the other man who had been knocked off his horse would never get up again. Neither would the two men who had been hit just outside the cabin door. So far as Quint could see, all the others had escaped.

The wounded man was Jules. Apparently, Slade had recognized him. That explained why he had risked exposing himself to get to him. Slade jerked the wounded man to his feet and half dragged him toward the corral fence. As much as he disliked Jules and the things he had done, Quint felt sorry for him now. That was no way to treat a wounded man, no matter how bad he was. But one look at Slade's face and his blazing eyes warned Quint not to interfere.

Quint went to each of the three dead men. But all were men he had never seen before. If Judd and Blix Hurley or Cole Fray had been with Jules, they had escaped. According to Lem Baxter's information, they belonged to Jules' gang. But they might not have been here this morning.

Baxter and Benson came up the slope from the willows now. It was obvious that the escaped outlaws were not coming back to renew the battle. Quint went to meet them. Up by the corral, he saw Slade tying Jules to the big post at the corner of the corral. That was inhuman treatment, with Jules wounded as he was, but Quint didn't feel like bucking Slade himself in defense of Jules.

"Slade's a madman," Baxter said, panting from his climb up the slope. "Jules is half dead now. Why torture him more?"

"Look!" Benson exclaimed, pointing toward the corral.

Quint wheeled toward the corral just in time to see Slade, with a quick snap of his long knife, slice an ear off Jules' head. Jules' scream reached the far corners of the valley. Before any of the three shocked men could make a move to interfere, Slade had sliced off Jules' other ear.

Slade stepped back from Jules, his laugh mingling with Jules' screams and sobs. Quint felt sick. He hadn't known anyone could treat another human being like that.

"He said he'd cut off his ears," Lem Baxter said softly. "But I just didn't think he'd actually do it."

"What kind of a man is he?" Benson asked in awe.

"He carries a lot of hate inside him," Baxter said. "We've got to stop him before he butchers Jules inch by inch."

Quint started up the slope toward the corral with Baxter and Benson, but before they had gone ten feet, a shot rang out and a splinter was ripped from the top pole of the corral fence just a foot from Slade. Slade dodged around the corner of the corral, and Quint wheeled toward the sound of the shot. Quint realized instantly that one of the outlaws, at least, had returned and was trying to rescue Jules.

"There he is!" Baxter yelled, pointing toward the willows along the creek.

Quint had his gun in his hand and squeezed the trigger. His first shot missed, but it turned the outlaw's gun on him. Quint dodged down the slope, seeking cover from the outlaw's gun. Baxter went the other way down the slope, firing occasionally at the willows where the outlaw had disappeared.

Quint reached the trees without being hit. He raised his head to try to locate the gunman and almost got it torn off as a bullet slapped into a tree branch only an inch from his ear.

Quint saw the man then, just a few yards away, much closer than he had expected. The man ducked back into the trees, and Quint fired at the spot where he thought he should be. There was a yell, the little trees shook, then all was quiet.

Quint moved forward cautiously. He could be blundering into a perfect trap if the outlaw was faking an injury. But through the willows, Quint saw the man stretched out. Quint still hadn't gotten a good look at him. He only knew that he must be one of Jules' most loyal men, for he had been trying to get to Jules to save him from Slade.

Then Quint reached the man. He caught his breath as he recognized Blix Hurley. Of all the men with Jules, Quint would have expected almost any of them to come back and fight quicker than Blix. Apparently, Blix's loyalty to Jules was stronger than any loyalty he had ever known before.

Quint knelt and ran his fingers through Blix's pockets after he had made sure that his bullet had done its work. Lem Baxter came up as Quint was working.

Suddenly, Quint's fingers touched a small fold of paper; he drew it out into the early morning sunlight. Before he had completely unfolded it, he knew he had found what he had been looking for. He certainly hadn't expected Blix to have the other half of Joe Linzy's note. But this was it in his hand.

FIFTEEN

Quint spread out the paper. It was worn so badly that he could barely make out the words. He had to study it carefully.

is under the
he northwest
Mike's old
t to the stage
on't let Mike
et it.

Quint studied the note for a while. This didn't make any more sense than the half he had. He was sure that Fray couldn't have made out anything from it either.

He unbuckled his belt so he could get to the waistband of his pants where he had hidden his half of the note. He couldn't understand why Fray had entrusted Blix Hurley with the half note. Fray must have expected Quint to try to take it from him and had decided that the safest place for it was with someone else. Quint hadn't realized that Fray and Blix Hurley were such close partners.

"Something important?" Lem Baxter asked as Quint worked.

Quint had almost forgotten Baxter in his haste to get the other half of the note. Quint quickly told him about the note, skipping all the details. He took his half out of its hiding place and moved to a smooth rock. There he spread out the two pieces and fitted them together. The words, now faded, were hard to read:

The money	is under the
floor in t	he northwest
corner of	Mike's old
cabin nex	t to the stage
station. D	on't let Mike
see you g	et it.

"It's right there at the station in Julesburg!" Quint exclaimed in amazement.

"What's Mike got to do with it?" Baxter mused.

"I don't know. Maybe nothing. This note must have been meant for Gilda if Joe Linzy didn't get back to get the money himself. The note says not to let Mike see her get the money."

Cole Fray and Judd Hurley suddenly stepped out of the willows behind Quint's back.

"The other half of the note finally came to light, I see," Fray said. "Go ahead, Quint. Make a funny move. All I want is an excuse."

"Your friend, Slade, doesn't even need an excuse to butcher a man," Judd said.

Quint hadn't moved; he knew he didn't dare

to if he wanted to live. He doubted if either Judd Hurley or Cole Fray would have any more compunctions about shooting a man than Jack Slade had.

"Stand up real easy, Quint," Fray said. "Then back away from that rock."

Quint obeyed slowly, glancing at Baxter. Baxter was under Judd's gun. He looked up the slope to the corral. Benson was there, apparently trying to convince Slade to use some humanity. But Slade was getting his revenge for the wounds Jules had given him, and he was brushing Benson off like he would a bothersome fly. It looked to Quint as if Slade was deliberately nicking Jules with each bullet he fired, but not wounding him seriously with any shot.

But Quint had his own troubles now. Fray wanted the two halves of the note, and he would get them. But what would he do then? With all the killing around them, Fray and Judd would surely kill Quint and Baxter, too. Quint knew that Judd wanted him dead. He'd never have a better chance to get the job done.

Fray moved over to the rock and scooped up the two pieces of paper and stuffed them into his pocket without taking his eyes off Quint. Quint could see Slade up at the corral from where he stood. He saw Jules suddenly sag against the ropes holding him to the corral post and guessed that Slade had finally killed him.

“Let’s get it over with,” Judd said, and Quint had no doubt what he meant.

Quint considered trying to make a fight of it. He wouldn’t have a chance, but even that would be better than dying like a dog.

But Quint hadn’t counted on Slade. Now that his game with Jules was over, Slade turned his attention to other things. He didn’t hesitate an instant when he saw the drama in the edge of the willows below him. His gun, which he had just reloaded, began roaring again.

Cole Fray and Judd Hurley suddenly forgot their immediate goal of killing their two captives. Their guns roared in response to Slade’s gun, but they were already on the move back into the trees.

Slade didn’t ease up. He came down the slope on the run, his gun barking at steady intervals. As soon as Fray and Judd disappeared into the willows, Quint reached for his gun again. But the two men had melted into the thick trees. A minute later Quint heard the pound of horses’ hoofs.

Slade and Benson reached them then. “Those outlaws we flushed out of the cabin are probably scattered over the whole area by now,” Benson said.

“I’ll run them down,” Slade promised.

“Those two that just pulled out will head for Julesburg as fast as they can ride,” Quint said.

"I've got to beat them there. When is the next stage east?"

"Not for several hours," Slade said. "If they're trying to get to Julesburg ahead of you, they'll head straight east. It's a lot shorter than the stage route."

Quint had thought of that. But the two outlaws were on horses without saddles. They hadn't had time to cinch on saddles when they left their corral this morning.

"I'm going to trail them," Quint decided. "Anybody going with me?"

"I got the man I really wanted," Slade said. "But now I've got the rest of this gang to corral or run out of the country. You can take the horses you rode out here. Send them back to me from Julesburg the first chance you get."

As they made their way back through the trees to the horses, Quint thought that he shouldn't have any trouble catching up with Judd and Fray or beating them to Julesburg if they escaped him. A man couldn't ride too many miles bareback without any supplies. He certainly couldn't move as fast as a man with a good saddle and food and water.

But when they reached their horses they discovered that two of the ones they had ridden out from the station this morning were gone. In their places were two barebacked ones.

"They stole our horses, too!" Baxter exclaimed.

“It’s a wonder they didn’t take all of them,” Quint said.

“The dirty horse thieves!” Slade exclaimed. “Take one of the saddled horses, Quint. I can get plenty of saddles up at the corral for the others.”

“Who’s going with me?” Quint asked.

“I am,” Baxter said quickly.

“Somebody’s got to stay and do a lot of burying,” Benson said. “I’ll take care of that, then come on to Julesburg on the stage. That many miles on the back of a horse doesn’t exactly appeal to me.”

Quint checked the lunch in the saddlebags and the water in the canteens before mounting. He found the tracks left by Judd and Cole Fray in the wet grass. They were headed east. But the trail would be mighty hard to follow once the dew burned off the grass.

Quint didn’t know how far it was straight across the prairie to Julesburg, but he was sure it was over a hundred and fifty miles. It might be a long chase, but they had to catch Fray and Judd or beat them to Julesburg.

As Quint expected, once the dew was gone, the tracks disappeared. But Fray and Judd had left no doubt about their course—straight east, the shortest route to Julesburg. Quint found it hard to hold down the pace. But these horses had a long way to go, and there was little chance that Quint and Baxter could get any fresh horses between here and Julesburg unless they dropped down along the stage line. That was too far out of their way. The stage line took a deep swing to the south between the station, where they had gotten the horses, and Julesburg. It cut through La Porte and down the Poudre River to Latham where it joined the South Platte. From there it ran east and northeast to Julesburg.

When Quint and Lem Baxter came to a creek late in the afternoon, they stopped to let the horses drink and rest. They refilled their canteens and ate some food. Then they remounted and pushed on to the east. Quint was disappointed. He hadn't caught sight of Judd and Fray since they started on the chase. But he knew they were ahead somewhere.

Quint didn't call a halt until long after dark. They were back in the saddle again before daylight. Quint paced their progress according to the endurance of the horses.

Toward the end of the second day, Quint began to veer a little to his right. If he had been wrong in his course, he could correct it by swerving to the south where he would find the South Platte. He could follow the river right into Julesburg. Anyway, their horses were thirsty as well as gaunt from lack of grazing time. It had been a grueling two days.

They came to the river late at night; Quint, despite his impatience, knew they had to rest.

He let the horses have water, then picketed them to graze in the deep grass. Quint and Baxter dropped off to sleep, too tired to worry about posting a guard.

But they were up and in the saddle once more before daylight. Now they followed the stage road on the south side of the river. Quint hadn't been over this road enough to be sure just how far they were from Julesburg. But he soon found that they were closer than he had thought. They rode into the station well before noon with horses too exhausted to be worth much for a long time.

Quint looked for Mike Shield at the barn, but he didn't see him. A sudden fear gripped him. Had they been too late despite their desperate race across the prairie?

Quint loosened the cinch on his horse and left him at the watering trough in the corral. Baxter did the same, apparently struck by the same feeling that obsessed Quint.

They ran to Mike's cabin, just beyond the corrals. Quint got there ahead of Baxter and pushed open the door. One glance told him that they were too late. The interior of the cabin was a shambles. The floor in the northwest corner of the one-room cabin was torn up; dirt had been scooped from under the floor and thrown over the rest of the room. The table was upset, and the grass tick jerked from the bed.

Quint didn't understand that. The note had said the money was buried under the floor in the northwest corner of the cabin. Why had Fray and Judd torn up the bed and upset the table?

It struck Quint then that perhaps Mike Shield had put up a struggle. Quint pushed into the room, looking for Mike. He found him in the southwest corner, an overturned chair lying on him.

Quint jerked the chair away. He suddenly felt sick. He'd seen another man beaten just like this—Joe Linzy. Cole Fray had done that. Apparently, Fray had done this, too. But why had Mike put up such a struggle?

Baxter kneeled beside Quint. "Is he alive?"

As if the sound of Baxter's voice had roused him, Mike groaned. Quint grabbed a pillow from the bunk and put it under his head. His face was badly battered, but Quint doubted if that was his most serious injury.

Mike opened his eyes, but for a moment they didn't focus on anything.

"I'd better get the doc," Baxter said.

Mike's eyes came down to Quint's face then. "No," he whispered. "I want to tell you something."

Quint glanced up at Baxter. Baxter nodded and got to his feet. He hurried out after the doctor. Quint knew that Mike's slim chances of surviving depended on his being quiet. But Mike had something to say, and Quint knew he would say it or die trying. So he didn't even suggest that Mike be quiet.

"Was it Cole Fray who beat you up?" he asked.

"Yes," Mike said. "He wanted the money my son buried in this cabin."

"Your son?" Quint exclaimed.

"He called himself Joe Linzy," Mike whispered. "Him and Fray and Spark held up a bank. But Joe took all the money. He hid it here. I didn't know about it till I accidentally found it. I have two other kids back east. Both need money bad so I sent it to them. Joe stole it; he shouldn't have had it, anyway."

"Why didn't Joe tell you about the money?" Quint asked.

For a minute, Mike stared unseeingly at the ceiling. Quint thought he hadn't heard. But then he answered.

"Joe didn't trust nobody, not even me or his girl. He was a good boy once, but he went bad when he got in with Fray. I made sure he didn't get to use his stolen money. Fray won't get it either."

Mike sank back on the pillow; for a moment, Quint thought he was dead. But then he saw that he was still breathing, but it was shallow and little more than gasps. Baxter came back on the run to report that the doctor was out at the edge of town on a call. He'd come as soon as he got back.

"It will be too late then, won't it?" he said, looking at Mike.

"Afraid so," Quint agreed.

Gilda came running in. "What happened?" she demanded. "I saw Lem run up to Doc's office and back."

Quint nodded at Mike. Quint knew now that Mike would say no more. Fray had killed his second man by beating him to death.

"Did you know he was Joe Linzy's father?" Quint asked.

Gilda nodded and turned to look out the one window. "Nobody else knew it except Cole Fray. Mike told me after you left that Fray had been threatening him if he didn't tell him where Joe hid the money."

"So that's why Mike was so sure he'd be killed," Quint said. "He knew that when Fray found out the money was gone, he'd kill him just for spite. Did he tell you what he had done with the money?"

Gilda nodded. "Yesterday," she said. "I was mad enough at first to beat him to death myself. But after I thought about it, I didn't blame him. His other kids needed the money, and Joe was already dead."

"Fray ought to swing for this," Baxter said, looking at Mike Shield.

“I think Cole and Judd are still in town,” Gilda said. “I saw them ride in and leave their horses in front of the station.”

“Where are they now?” Quint asked, looking at Mike and feeling the fury build up in him.

“I don’t know,” she said. “Ordinarily I wouldn’t even have seen them. I’m usually asleep that time of day. But I was so worked up over what Mike told me about the money being gone that I couldn’t sleep well. That’s why I heard them when they rode in.”

Quint’s attention was caught suddenly by a man dodging out the back door of the station. The man looked around frantically, then ran toward the little cabin behind the corrals. Quint recognized the station agent.

“What’s wrong?” he demanded as the agent stumbled in the door.

“It’s Hurley and Fray,” the agent panted. “They robbed the station and tied me up. They’re planning to sack the town.”

SIXTEEN

It took a moment for the full significance of the agent's words to strike Quint. In a town no bigger than Julesburg, two desperate men, well-armed, with no compunction against killing anyone who got in their way, could clean out the town and vanish into the wide prairie in any direction.

Maybe they hadn't figured on Quint and Lem Baxter getting back this soon. By tying up the station agent, they had eliminated a big part of the probable opposition. On the other hand, maybe they did know that Quint was back. They surely knew that Quint and Baxter had been right behind them all the way from the mountains.

"What about my store?" Baxter said, breaking into Quint's thoughts. "Mary is up there alone. Unless Mrs. Hurley is there helping her."

Quint wheeled to look up the street. But the buildings between the little cabin and the street blocked his view. Judd might know how he felt about Mary Baxter. Caution was the one way to deal with Judd and Fray. But if Mary and Quint's mother were in danger, caution would be a luxury that Quint's anger couldn't tolerate.

Suddenly, Quint turned back to the agent. "If you were tied, how did you get loose?"

"Fray tied me," the agent said. "He was in a

hurry and madder than any man I ever saw. He wasn't too careful."

"What did he say? Where did they go from the station?"

The agent dropped down on the bare springs of the bed. "Fray kept mumbling about getting a fortune if he had to kill everybody in Julesburg to get it. Hurley didn't say much, just that he had some killing to do before he left. I figured sure they'd kill me."

"They didn't have anything against you," Quint said. "But they have against others here."

"They'll hit my store sure," Baxter said. "They know I was with Slade on that raid. And you killed Blix, Dan. Judd will be after you."

Quint nodded. "He was after me before. He won't leave town now until he makes his try. I'm going after him, and Fray too. Any man who will beat a man to death has to be killed like a mad dog."

"I'm going to the store," Baxter said. "I don't want them to get their hands on Mary."

"Ma may be there, too, helping Mary," Quint said. "If Judd gets his hands on either one of them, he'll know I'll come after him."

Gilda stayed with the agent while Quint and Baxter left the cabin and ran up the alley behind the blacksmith shop. Quint tried to figure where Fray and Judd would strike after leaving the stage station. He didn't even know how long ago they had left the agent tied up there.

They would be sure to try to rob the store, but they would know that Mary Baxter would be there. If they found Mrs. Hurley there too, they might just hole up in the store and wait to ambush Quint and Lem Baxter. They'd have a better chance of gunning them down without any risk to themselves.

There was no sound from the rear of the blacksmith shop, as they passed. Quint wondered fleetingly about that. Maybe the blacksmith, Mason, had already been overpowered by the two men. That was likely, Quint thought, because with Mason out of the picture, the two outlaws would just about have the town in their hands.

Quint caught Baxter's arm and stopped him as he heard some sound out in the street. When their own running stopped, Quint clearly heard the patter of running feet. But it was not the heavy running of a man. Quint ducked into the rear of the blacksmith shop and ran to the front door.

As he reached the front of the shop, he saw a boy racing down the street toward the stage station. He recognized little Billy Mason, the blacksmith's son. Quint whistled softly and the boy stopped as if he'd been struck by a pole.

"In here, Billy," Quint said in a loud whisper.

The boy turned and dived inside the blacksmith shop.

"Where are you going?" Quint demanded.

Trembling, the boy just panted for a moment as he looked at Quint and Lem Baxter, who had followed Quint in the back door.

"It's those two men," he said finally. "They've got guns. They're going to kill everybody in town."

"Where are they?"

"They're in the store. They came in here and took Pa and me and made us go over to the store with them. They tied up Pa."

"Who else do they have there?" Baxter demanded.

"Miss Mary and Mrs. Hurley. They were working in the store."

"How did they happen to let you go?" Quint asked.

"They told me to go down to the station and see if you were there," the boy said. "If you were, I was to tell you they had Miss Mary and Mrs. Hurley and were going to beat them to death like they did Mike Shield. You—" The boy choked on his fright. "You were to come up and watch."

Quint shot a look at Baxter. The usually mild face of the storekeeper was drawn into a tense mask of fury and determination. Quint couldn't quite believe that Judd and Fray would actually beat the two women. They had sent that word with the boy to make Quint and Lem Baxter make a foolish dash toward the store to rescue them. If they did, Judd and Fray could pick them off like shooting fish in a barrel.

But Quint could see that Lem Baxter wasn't sure that Fray wouldn't beat the women. He hadn't forgotten how Mike Shield had looked dying from the beating Fray had administered. Quint reached out and touched Baxter's arm.

"Take it easy, Lem. They're just trying to make us do something foolish."

"That's my daughter down in that store," Baxter said thickly.

"She means a lot to me, too," Quint reminded him. "And so does my mother. But I want to stay alive to help them. Neither one of us will do them any good if we rush out there and let Judd and Cole Fray fill us full of lead."

Baxter took a deep breath. "You're right. But how can we get at them?"

"We can't smoke them out with bullets," Quint said. "They'll likely put the women up next to the windows and doors, so if we do rush them and get through their bullets, we'll be shooting the women when we break in, not Judd and Fray."

"They're probably watching both the front and back doors," Baxter said.

Quint nodded. "You have a small window in your north bedroom, don't you? Is it fastened?"

"Not likely," Baxter said. "If it is, a man could break the fastener. But how are we going to get around to it? It's on the north side of the building and we're on the south."

"That's the only reason we can get there," Quint said, an idea rapidly taking shape in his mind. Baxter had built his store, unlike most store buildings, with two windows on either side to let in more light. "We'll let them know we're here in the blacksmith shop. We'll start shooting through the store windows. But we have to aim high. We don't want to hit Mary or Ma or Mason."

"They won't aim high when they shoot back," Baxter said. "What good is that going to do? We'll just be pinned down here. They won't come out after us. They hold all the cards."

"We don't want them to come out," Quint said. "We'll find a good place for you to hide, like behind this forge. From here you can shoot through one of the shop's windows toward one of the windows of the store. If you stay down behind the forge, they can't hit you. I'll slip out the back way and around by the stage station and warehouse, then up behind the boarding house and saloon. I might be able to get to the north side of your store without them seeing me if you keep them busy here."

The boy had been listening with mouth open. "I'll get Pa's gun," he said now. "I can shoot through the other window once in a while. They'll think you're both here."

Quint nodded. "Good idea, Billy. We'll find

a place where a bullet can't get through to you. Just remember—aim high."

As soon as Baxter fired the first shot, an answering shot came through the window of the blacksmith shop, proving that the two outlaws had seen the boy duck into the blacksmith shop.

Billy fired his father's gun through the other window; an answering bullet came through that window. It was lucky, Quint thought, that Mason had made two windows on that side of his shop for ventilation.

Quint hurried, out the back door and turned toward the stage station. He had no real fear for Baxter or the Mason boy. Judd and Fray wouldn't leave the store. They had the two women as hostages. As long as they were sure the two were in the blacksmith shop, they'd sit tight and wait for Quint or Baxter to make the first break.

Quint reached the station and went through the back door and out the front. Here he came to grips with his first problem. He had to cross the street to the warehouse. He was sure that the men in the store down the street couldn't hit him from that distance. Surprise was the only real weapon he had. He didn't dare let them see him or they'd be waiting for him when he got to the store, and that would be the end.

Fray's and Judd's horses were standing at the hitchrack. Neither was tied; the reins were just draped over the bar. Apparently, Fray and Judd had been in a big hurry when they rode up here. It gave Quint an idea.

He turned the horses toward the warehouse and started them across the street. Crouching on the far side, he moved along with them until he reached the warehouse. Judd and Fray were sure to see the horses crossing the street. But they wouldn't be likely to notice a man's legs moving with the horses' legs. They'd remember that they hadn't tied their horses and think the animals were just wandering across the street.

Once behind the warehouse, Quint began running, dodging from the warehouse to the rear of the tall boarding house. From there, he had to cross the alley to the back of the saloon. For just a moment, he was in sight of the store across the street. But from the steady shooting, he guessed that both Judd and Fray were occupied with the shots from the blacksmith shop.

He thought of the beating he had taken from Fray behind the saloon shortly after he arrived in Julesburg. But revenge for that beating was only a small coal in the burning fury that drove him toward Fray and Judd now.

At the street corner of the saloon, he hesitated. The shots were still booming steadily from the store and the blacksmith. Here Quint had to trust to luck. If either of the two men in the store happened to turn and look out the front into the street just as he was running across, they'd see him and his surprise would be ruined.

Ducking low, Quint sped across the street to the corner of the store. He detected no change in the steady hammering of the guns on the far side. He was sure he had made it undetected. He ran down the length of the building to the window that opened into the bedroom.

He tried the window and found that it wasn't even fastened. It pulled open on its hinges without a sound. As quietly as possible, Quint climbed through the opening that wasn't meant for a man his size. But he made it and found himself in Lem Baxter's bedroom.

He crossed the room quietly and slowly opened the door. He checked his gun and held it in his hand, ready for instant use as he moved out into the main room of the Baxter living quarters.

He saw no one. From the sounds out front, he guessed that Judd and Cole Fray were still firing from the store windows.

Quint moved to the doorway that separated the living quarters from the store. He pulled the door slightly open to see through. But here his good luck failed him. The door squealed right during a lull in the firing.

He saw a movement at the first window and jerked the door open so he could get a better view. Judd was at the closest window. Fray was at the other window. He caught a glimpse of his mother close to Judd. He didn't see Mary or the blacksmith that Billy Mason said was tied up here in the store.

Judd fired even as he was wheeling. His bullet slammed into the door jamb, splintering it. Quint fired more slowly, taking time to make sure he wouldn't hit his mother. Judd rocked backward as the bullets struck him.

Quint felt a sharp slap at his shoulder before he could turn to face Fray. Fray's bullet hadn't missed, although it hadn't hit where Fray had intended.

Quint spun toward Fray, firing twice. Fray dived away from the window toward the front door. Quint thought he had hit Fray, but he wasn't sure. Fray fired another shot at Quint that missed. Quint fired back, then ducked behind a barrel to reload.

There were no more shots. Quint took only time enough to load two chambers in his gun. Then he ducked across the aisle of the store, looking for Judd. He found him crumpled under the window. One close look told him he had nothing more to fear from him.

He ran to the door, holding his wounded arm tightly against his side. Already the pain was beginning to rip through the wound. He didn't see Fray outside. When he heard his mother calling him, he turned back.

Ann Hurley was still close to the window where Judd had made her stay. Quint's anger soared when he saw the ropes that were holding his mother to the chair by the window. He flipped the ropes off and let her up.

"Where's Mary?" he asked.

"Didn't you see?" Ann Hurley exclaimed. "Cole Fray took her with him."

Quint wheeled toward the front door again. He didn't know where Fray would be. He'd probably be lying in wait somewhere for Quint. But Quint was beyond caring about that. He had to kill Cole Fray somehow. He wouldn't rest until either he or Fray was dead.

He ran outside, suddenly fighting a wave of nausea that swept over him. He shook it off and stepped off the porch. His shoulder was beginning to throb with a sickening pain. But he had to find Fray and rescue Mary. He looked down the alley between the store and the blacksmith shop. There was no one there.

Baxter came out of the shop. "Fray got away," he said. "He had somebody with him."

"It was Mary," Quint said. "Where did he go?"

"Across the street into the saloon."

Quint turned and ran toward the saloon, holding his arm tightly against his side and gritting his teeth against the pain. But there was only the bartender in the saloon.

"Where did Fray go?"

"Out the back," the bartender said. "He was bleeding from a busted arm."

"Good," Quint said and ran on out the back. Apparently, Fray was in as bad shape as he was.

Quint looked up and down the back of the buildings. Fray could have gone toward the river, but Quint guessed he had stayed in town. He might have ducked into the boarding house. If so, he would be hard to dig out of there.

But Mrs. Ketrick was at the back door when Quint came by. She had a shotgun cradled in her arm.

"He headed for the stage station," she said. "He wanted in here, but I wouldn't let him in."

"Why didn't you shoot him?" Quint demanded.

"I ain't no murderer," Mrs. Ketrick said indignantly. "But I sure wasn't going to let him turn my boarding house into a battlefield, either."

Quint ran on, knowing that the stage station would be Fray's last stand. There was no place beyond it to go except the corrals and Mike's old cabin.

Quint reached the corner of the warehouse and stood there, fighting off another wave of nausea. Then, cocking his gun, he started across the street toward the station, knowing that Fray had to make his stand soon.

Quint saw him leap out the front door where he could get a good shot at Quint. Quint's finger tightened on the trigger then stopped. Fray was holding Mary with his good arm. His other arm wasn't broken as the bartender had thought, for he held his gun in that hand.

He fired, but apparently his arm wasn't as steady as it should have been. The bullet snapped past Quint's head. But still Quint didn't dare fire. He might hit Mary.

He knew he should duck for cover. But his rage at the advantage Fray was taking kept him from acting sensibly. He kept on running toward Fray. Fray fired again and missed.

Then, when Quint was within twenty feet of Fray, another gun roared and Fray threw up his hands and stumbled away from Mary. Quint's gun roared, almost from a reflex action, the bullet slamming into Fray. His fingers had been aching to squeeze the trigger from the moment Fray had appeared.

Fray spun around and crumpled in a heap. Quint didn't need to examine him to know he wouldn't get up. Mary ran to him, sobbing almost hysterically. Quint used his good arm to pull her to him.

Over Mary's shoulder, Quint saw Gilda come out the front door of the station, a gun in her hand. She stared down at Fray's body then looked up at Quint.

"I owed him that and more for beating Joe to death."

She turned and went back inside. Mary caught her breath and stepped back, quickly regaining her composure.

“We must doctor that arm, Dan. Come on inside.”

Quint felt heady and was sure it wasn’t all dizziness from his wound. “I’ll come if you’ll promise me you’ll give me a hug like that every night when I get home from work.”

She looked startled for a moment then laughed. “I’ll do it, if that’s the way you want it.”

“That’s the way I want it,” he said emphatically.

Center Point Large Print
600 Brooks Road / PO Box 1
Thorndike, ME 04986-0001 USA

(207) 568-3717

US & Canada:
1 800 929-9108
www.centerpointlargeprint.com